The Immigrants' Chronicles

FROM CHINA TO AMERICA

THE JOURNEY OF
Yung Lee

JUDITH McCOY-MILLER

Be sure to read all the books in
The Immigrants' Chronicles

The Journey of Emilie
The Journey of Hannah
The Journey of Pieter and Anna
The Journey of Elisa
The Journey of Yung Lee

Cook Communications Ministries,
Colorado Springs, Colorado 80918
Cook Communications, Paris, Ontario
Kingsway Communications, Eastbourne, England

THE JOURNEY OF YUNG LEE
© 2000 by Judith McCoy-Miller

Edited by Kathy Davis
Design by PAZ Design Group and Dana Sherrer of iDesignEtc.
Art direction by Kelly S. Robinson
Cover illustration by Cheri Bladholm

First printing, 2000
Printed in the United States of America
04 03 02 01 00   5 4 3 2 1

Library of Congress Cataloging-in-Publication Data

McCoy-Miller, Judith.
    The journey of Yung Lee : from China to America / Judith McCoy-Miller.
    p. cm. :— (The immigrants' chronicles)
    Summary: In the mid 1800s, after reluctantly leaving China for America with
her older brother, her only living relative, twelve-year-old Lee endures many
hardships through her strong Christian faith.
    ISBN 0-7814-3285-5
    [1. Emigration and immigration—Fiction. 2. Ocean travel—Fiction.
3. Orphans—Fiction. 4. Brothers and sister—Fiction. 5. Christian life—
Fiction.] I. Title. II. Series.

PZ7.M1377 Jo 2000
[Fic]—dc21   99-041982

DEDICATION

To my prayer warrior, my friend, my sister—
Mary Kay Woodford

Chapter One

CANTON, CHINA 1854

Several tears escaped Yung Lee's almond-shaped eyes. They glistened on her golden cheeks as they rolled downward and plopped onto her blue cotton shirt.

"Try to chase away your sadness, Lee. I know it's difficult, but you must try," Mrs. Conroy said, taking a white lace handkerchief from her pocket and wiping away the twelve-year-old girl's tears.

"Why must I try? I don't want to go to America. Is there nothing you can do?" Lee begged while wrapping her small arms around Mrs. Conroy.

"You know I talked to your brother! I even promised Yung Fong that you could stay with us at the compound until he returns from California. He wouldn't hear of it," Mrs. Conroy answered, pulling Lee close to give her a big bear hug.

Lee loved the way Mrs. Conroy smelled—like a garden full of blooming flowers. From the first time she had snuggled close to the good-natured American woman almost four years ago, Lee had never grown tired of her sweet scent. And handkerchiefs—Lee loved the way Mrs. Conroy always had a handkerchief tucked deep in her pocket, ready to wipe away a tear or clean a stubborn smudge of dirt. She loved the way Mrs. Conroy laughed, her soft, melodic voice rippling through the air like wind chimes tinkling in a soft breeze. With her gentle, loving spirit, Mrs. Conroy had soothed Lee's sorrow and fierce yearning for her own family. Holding Lee close, she would comfort her throughout the long nights—nights when Lee would weep bitter tears for her mother, father, three brothers, and two sisters, who had all died in a territorial rebellion. Yes, Lee loved Mrs. Conroy—from the top of her head to the tip of her toes; she loved everything about her.

"Fong won't let me stay in China because he's never coming back!" Lee declared.

"Oh, I think ..."

"No! I know my brother. He tells you and me that he's going to stay in California only until he becomes rich. I think he even tells himself that. But deep inside," Lee said, pointing to her heart, "he has no plan to return to China."

"Lee, I understand. You're upset and frightened. Leaving everything you know to go to a strange land with different customs and strange people is very difficult. But you're a strong girl. If you will try to make this into an opportunity instead of a punishment, I think you will be much happier," Mrs. Conroy recommended calmly.

"The only thing that would make me happy is to have my brother say that I can remain in China," Lee stubbornly replied. "It's not fair. Fong always gets to decide what happens in my life."

"Well, he's responsible for you. He's older and ..."

"Wiser? I don't think so. He thinks that just because he's a boy he knows everything!"

"He's twenty-three, and I think that qualifies him to be called a man. You must remember that he has learned a lot in those years."

"That doesn't mean he's always right. Besides, sometimes he acts more like a boy than a man."

Mrs. Conroy smiled. "I suppose that's true. Sometimes I act more like a little girl than a woman. It's lots more fun."

Lee returned the smile. "I still think I should be able to decide where I live."

"Fong's done a pretty good job so far, wouldn't you agree?"

"Well, I didn't want to leave our home in the country, but he made me. And I hated living in Canton. At least until Fong brought me here to live with you," she quickly added. "Living with you was a good decision. So why can't he just leave me here? He thought it was a good idea four years ago."

"It's not the same, Lee. While both of you have been living in Canton, Fong could visit you every day, and the two of you got to go places together. Permitting you to remain with us when he sails off for the United States is a horse of a different color."

"Horse of a different color—what's that mean?" Lee asked, a look of confusion etched on her face.

"It's an old saying, something like one of your Chinese proverbs. It means that Fong's earlier approval for you to live with us is totally different from permitting you to remain in China while he lives in another country," she explained.

"Well, I don't like that different-colored horse," Lee replied.

Mrs. Conroy laughed. "Try to understand how he is thinking. The two of you are all that remain of the Yung family. He loves you and wants his family with him."

"I understand that. I want to be with him also. But I want to be with him in China, not in California! Besides, I don't care if we're rich."

"Fong wants to provide a good life for you, and he doesn't think he can do that in China. He sees an opportunity in California to make a better life for both of you."

"Why are you taking his side? I thought you were my friend."

Mrs. Conroy smiled and patted Lee's hand. "I am your friend, Lee, and I'm not taking his side. I'm trying to help you understand. For a long time after I went to bed last night, I couldn't fall asleep. While I was lying there, I began thinking back to the day I sailed from America to make my home in China."

"But you wanted to come to China," Lee argued.

"Oh, no, but I didn't. I tried and tried to convince

Mr. Conroy that he should be a preacher at a big church in Boston. But he wouldn't hear of it," she explained.

Lee frowned, folded her arms, and shook her head back and forth. "He should have listened to you."

Laughing, she tousled Lee's shiny black hair and then let her arm drop around the girl's shoulders. "No. He was right. God called Mr. Conroy to be a missionary in China. I was wrong to try to persuade him to go against God's direction."

"That's a horse of a different color, too, because God didn't tell Fong to go to California. Fong doesn't even believe in our God," Lee retorted.

"You certainly caught onto that horse thing in a hurry! But you are right. I know Fong isn't leaving because he wants to serve God."

"Why didn't you just stay in Boston?" Lee asked.

"Because Mr. Conroy and I are a family, and my place is with him. At first I thought I would never be happy again. But now that I am here, I'm happier than I've ever been in my life. I love your beautiful country, I've learned many of your customs, and I've made some wonderful friends. And you will do the same thing in America. Your life is going to be a true adventure."

"You sound just like my brother. From the time I was born, we lived among soldiers fighting their awful battles in the countryside. Except for Fong, my whole family died because of their silly wars. I just want to stay here at the mission compound with you and be safe. I don't need any more adventure in my life," Lee answered bitterly.

"There is one thing I know for sure," Mrs. Conroy teased.

"What? Tell me, please."

"You are going to America with two very special gifts. Gifts that most Chinese people do not possess."

"What?" Lee asked, wondering how she could possibly have anything the rest of her people didn't possess.

"You go with the gift of Jesus, which means that you will

8

never be without a friend. When you think there is nobody who cares, you must remember that Jesus is always there, waiting to hear from you. And in the United States, you won't have to worry about telling people you're a Christian. You know how the Chinese officials dislike Americans, especially Christians who want to tell the Chinese people about Jesus?"

"Yes, I know. Fong told me I should never tell anyone I worship God. He doesn't think it's wise for any Chinese person to love Jesus," Lee replied softly.

"Well, that will no longer be a problem. That's one good thing about going to America, isn't it?" Mrs. Conroy encouraged.

"I guess you're right about that, but what's the other gift?" Lee asked, not totally convinced any of this made a difference.

"You can understand the English language. Do you know how wonderful that is?"

"I don't feel very wonderful," Lee replied honestly.

"Maybe not now. But when you go to school in the United States your life will be so much easier because you already know the language. All those lessons you've endured are going to pay off."

Lee gave her a feeble smile.

"Come on, Lee! You can do better than that! Your smile reminds me of a sick puppy," Mrs. Conroy said, making a face that caused both of them to giggle.

"You make me laugh, even when I don't want to," Lee said. "But that face you made at me looked more like a dead fish than a sick puppy!"

"Oh it did, did it? Well, I'll just have to spend a bit more time practicing my animal imitations."

The gloomy look had once again returned to Lee's eyes. "If we weren't leaving so soon, I could help you."

"Now don't you go getting that sick puppy look again! Would you like me to come and see you off?"

Lee's head bobbed up and down, her glossy dark hair falling forward over her face. "Yes, I would like that very much."

"Good. I would like that too," Mrs. Conroy said as she returned Lee's smile.

"Does California look like the European sector?" Lee asked, wanting to talk about something besides leaving Mrs. Conroy.

"I'm not sure. I've never been to California. I lived in a place called Boston, which is in a different part of the country."

Lee gave her a puzzled look. "But they look the same, don't they?"

"No, not at all. Let me see—how can I explain this? Even though Canton and Shanghai are both cities in China, they have many differences. Boston and San Francisco are both cities located in the United States, but they aren't the same."

Lee still looked confused. "But I've never been to Shanghai."

"Let me try to explain another way. Do you recall how the countryside looked when you were a small child living in the country?"

"Yes," Lee answered, shaking her head up and down while she pictured the lush greenery and flowering trees that covered the landscape in early spring.

"Then, after your parents died, your brother brought you here to Canton. And Canton looks very different from your home in the country. After a short time, your brother brought you here to the compound to stay with us. And the European sector looks very different from the rest of Canton, doesn't it?"

"I understand! All of these places you described are in China, but they all look different."

"Right! That's how it is in every country. From city to city, there are some contrasts in the customs and scenery."

"Do the houses and buildings in Boston look like the European sector?"

"A few. But this area looks more like a European city where the buildings are much fancier than those in American towns. That's why it's called the European sector," Mrs. Conroy explained.

"Hmmm. Do you think California looks like a Chinese city?"

"What? No, why do you ask?" Mrs. Conroy inquired.

"Your people built a city in China that looks like your country. Perhaps there is a town in California that looks like my country," Lee suggested.

"It's possible. I've heard that there is a Chinese community around the San Francisco area," Mrs. Conroy replied.

A smile spread across Lee's face. "If there is such a town, do you think Fong would agree to live there?" Lee asked, her excitement increasing. "That would make it much easier, don't you think?"

"Yes, but you know your brother's plans. He's determined to find gold, and I don't think you'll convince him."

"I know. That's all I hear him talk about—*Gam Saan*—the Gold Mountain. But I'll have time while we're on board the ship to try to change his mind," Lee retorted.

"That's true. But I don't think you should build your hopes upon changing Fong's plans. You'll only be disappointed and become angry with him if he doesn't agree with you," Mrs. Conroy cautioned, giving her small friend a knowing look.

"You think I should keep quiet and let him decide everything?" Lee questioned, the smile disappearing from her face.

"No, I didn't say that. It's all right to tell Fong how you feel and ask him to consider your wishes. But I think it would be wise if you spent your time considering how you will adjust to your new life and making plans to be happy wherever you are. There's a verse in the Bible, 1 Thessalonians 5:16-18, if my memory serves me correctly. It says that we should rejoice, pray without ceasing, and give thanks in every circumstance. I may not have quoted the verses exactly. But it means that even if we don't understand why certain things happen, God knows what is taking place, and we should try our very best to be joyful and thank Him for all He does—no matter how unfair our situations may seem," Mrs. Conroy explained.

"That's hard for someone who is only twelve years old," Lee replied.

Mrs. Conroy nodded her head in agreement. "It's hard no matter what your age."

Lee smiled. "I'll try to remember," she promised.

"Good! Now, let's have some lunch. I made rice with roasted duck, just the way you like it," Mrs. Conroy said as she began to carefully place the pink-flowered plates and cups on the table.

"Aren't we going to wait for Mr. Conroy?"

"I don't think he'll be back in time for lunch. But he promised to return before your brother arrives," Mrs. Conroy explained.

"Will you tell me more about your country while we eat?"

"I've been telling you about it for weeks. What other questions could you possibly have?"

"I have lots," she replied, taking small steps on her tiny bound feet as she followed behind Mrs. Conroy. "Sometimes I wish my feet hadn't been wrapped up to keep them small. Then I could walk as fast as you."

Mrs. Conroy gave her an encouraging smile. "But then you wouldn't be who you are—a member of the Yung family with strong Chinese traditions and ancestry."

At twelve years old, Lee was small for her age. Just over four feet tall, she was considered petite even among the people of her own country. What would the Americans think of someone so tiny—especially someone so small and with bound feet? "What if people in California don't like me?" Lee asked in a serious voice.

"That's a hard question. Do you remember when you first came to live with us? I talked to you about the differences in our appearance—you with your beautiful almond-shaped eyes, black hair, and golden skin. And me, with my blond hair, blue eyes, and pale skin?"

"And big feet," Lee added with a glint in her eye.

"Right! My very big feet," Mrs. Conroy agreed as she held her foot out.

"And me with my teeny-tiny feet," Lee said, pointing to her feet.

Mrs. Conroy laughed. "There are people from many places who have emigrated to the United States—from countries in Europe, Africa, Asia, South America—from all over the world. Some of them will look different; some will talk different . . ."

"But we are all God's creations, and He has given each of us special gifts," Lee said, finishing the sentence.

"Yes. Even if people make fun of you or refuse your friendship, you must always remember that you are special—that you look exactly the way God intended, and you are perfect in His sight."

"It's easy to believe that when everybody is nice to you. But if people are mean, I'm not so sure I'll remember," Lee said.

"I think you've learned that lesson very well, Lee. If someone says something mean to you, try to think of something kind to say. People are always surprised when you return their rude or angry remarks with kindness."

"I hope I don't have to find out. I hope everyone will be nice to me," Lee cheerfully responded. "Are you ready for more questions about the United States?"

"More questions? You've become such a little magpie during the years you've lived with us!"

"What's a magpie?"

Mrs. Conroy chuckled. "It's a bird that constantly makes a lot of noise. In the United States, people sometimes refer to folks who talk a lot as 'magpies.' And you'll have to admit that you've been talking a lot lately."

"So you think I sound like a cackling bird?" Lee asked, crossing her arms as she formed her face into a giant frown.

"I was teasing, Lee. I didn't mean to upset you," Mrs. Conroy said, rushing toward the girl.

"I know! And I was just teasing you when I acted unhappy," Lee replied, giggling.

"I see! So now you're doing imitations. You did a better job making me believe you were an upset girl than I did earlier today when I was imitating a sick puppy dog! But I'll have you know that magpies don't cackle. It's more of a screechy, annoying sound," she said, trying not to laugh.

"Screechy? You think I sound screechy?"

"I think you sound wonderful," Mrs. Conroy replied, grabbing her into a big hug. "And I'm going to miss you very much—screechy voice and all. Now, let's eat lunch before Fong gets here. I promised that you would be ready when he arrives."

Lee placed the wooden chopsticks between her fingers and began pushing the food around her plate. Each time Mrs. Conroy looked her way, she took a small bite, but her appetite had disappeared—and she feared that her life in China was soon going to disappear also.

Chapter Two

A sharp knock sounded at the door. "He's here," Lee whispered.

Mrs. Conroy nodded and pushed her chair away from the dining table. Lee kept her eyes riveted on Mrs. Conroy's back as she walked out of the room and toward the front door.

"We've been expecting you, Fong. Come in. Have you had your lunch?" she asked the thin, dark-haired young man.

"I'm not hungry. We must be on our way. Is she ready?" His excitement was evident.

"Yes, she's all packed. Would you mind if Mr. Conroy and I accompanied you to the river? Lee's not very happy right now, and I promised to go along."

"I know she doesn't want to leave Canton. Come on, Lee," he called, spotting his sister as she peeked around the doorway.

"Not without Mr. and Mrs. Conroy," she insisted.

"We must leave now. Come along!"

"Are you ready?" Mr. Conroy inquired as he bounded up the front stairs and into the entryway.

"If we don't leave immediately, we'll miss our boat," Fong explained.

"No need to worry. I've brought the horse and buggy around," Mr. Conroy replied. "We'll make it in plenty of time. Come on, Lee. I've already placed your belongings in the buggy." He swept her up into his arms.

Mr. Conroy was tall, and Lee always felt safe in his strong arms. When they went for walks or into the city, he would hold Lee high up in the air so that she could get a better view. But Lee knew that Mr. Conroy wasn't carrying her so that she could see some unusual spectacle or display. Today he was carrying her because Fong was in a hurry. The short walk to the buggy would take the rest of them no time at all. But it would be a slow journey for Lee on her tiny, tightly bound feet.

The warm breeze tugged at Lee's hair, blowing tiny wisps forward to tickle her nose. She was glad to see that Mr. Conroy had pushed back the top of the buggy. Mrs. Conroy probably asked him to fold the top down, Lee thought. Mrs. Conroy knew how much Lee liked to ride in the buggy and see all of the sights when they traveled about the city.

"I'll sit in back with Lee. Why don't you ride up front with Mr. Conroy?" Mrs. Conroy suggested to Fong while her husband assisted her into the buggy. After sitting down on the leather-cushioned seat, she wrapped her arm around Lee and pulled her close.

Fong nodded and pulled himself up beside Mr. Conroy. With a slap of the reins, the horse began moving down the street and out of the European sector heading toward the Deng River. The dapple-gray mare clopped along, passing rows of high walls that had been built to hide the homes and ornamental gardens of wealthy politicians.

"I always wish I could climb the walls and peek inside one of those houses," Mrs. Conroy confessed to her young friend.

"Me, too," Lee admitted. "I thought I was the only one!"

"No. In fact, even Mr. Conroy told me he would like to see inside," Mrs. Conroy confided, causing both of them to laugh.

As the buggy turned onto a busy street in the business district, Lee raised herself up while straining to take in the scene. She liked to see the traveling workmen conducting business along the streets. Spotting a man cooking vegetables and fish in a metal wok on his small portable grill, she sniffed deeply.

"It smells good, doesn't it?" Mrs. Conroy asked.

"Yes. Very good," Lee answered, wondering if people in California cooked on small stoves along the streets. They passed by a traveling repairer of umbrellas, a glassmender, and an ancient cobbler, all hard at work. A fortune-teller was sitting at a small table, attempting to lure customers as they passed by.

"Look, there's a barber," Lee said as the horse continued trotting down the street. A customer was perched on top of a small chest of drawers. They watched as the barber quickly finished shaving the top of his customer's head and then nimbly braided the man's remaining hair into a single plait, which fell down his back.

"I wish I could braid hair that quickly," Mrs. Conroy commented. "Look!" she urged, pointing toward a dentist who wore a string of teeth around his neck to advertise his trade. They all laughed when he gave them a toothless grin as they passed by.

"Do you think those are his teeth?" Mr. Conroy called from the front seat of the buggy.

"Eeew, what a terrible thought!" Lee declared. "I don't ever want him to pull one of my teeth."

"I don't think you need to worry. You're not going to be living here," Fong called back over his shoulder and then quickly turned around.

Lee stuck out her tongue and made a face at the back of his head when she thought no one was looking. She knew that Mrs. Conroy wouldn't approve and her brother would become angry over such behavior.

"You should show respect to your brother," Mrs. Conroy whispered in her ear.

Realizing that she'd been caught, Lee gave Mrs. Conroy a sheepish grin. "Well, he shouldn't be so mean," she whispered.

Mrs. Conroy nodded in agreement. "But you still need to show respect."

"I know," Lee replied, her shoulders slumping as she hung her head.

"Look! There's a peddler selling clay puppets," Mrs. Conroy excitedly pointed out.

Lee's sullen mood quickly vanished as she jiggled about, anxious to see the brightly colored puppets. Finally she saw the peddler and waved. He returned her smile and held one of the puppets high above the passing crowd for her to see. I'll probably never see clay puppets again, Lee thought, feeling a lump begin to form in her throat

"We need to hurry," Fong instructed Mr. Conroy when he pulled the horse and buggy to the side of the street, allowing two chairbearers carrying a sedan chair to pass by.

"We have ample time, and it's much kinder for us to wait on them. Would you want to wait if you were carrying that weight?"

"No," Fong admitted, with a note of shame in his voice as he watched the ornate chair balanced on long poles being carried by two men. Inside sat an elegantly dressed woman, most likely being transported to attend the theater with her husband or to visit a friend.

Slowly they moved onward, nearer and nearer to the river. Lee snuggled closer to Mrs. Conroy while they passed the warehouses and approached the factories that sat directly on the waterfront.

"I wonder why those factories don't topple into the water," Lee said, looking at the buildings that appeared to balance in mid-air.

"They're built on piles," Mr. Conroy explained. "When you get around to the other side, you'll see them. They're long, slender columns of wood that hold up the suspended portion of each building."

"You can pull the buggy over here," Fong said, pointing toward the side of the road. "I think that's our junk down there," he said, looking toward the large boat weaving in and out among the houseboats, lorchas, and sampans floating on the river.

"We'll be there in time," Mr. Conroy said in a soothing voice as he patted the young man on the back. "Why don't you get your sister's belongings, and I'll carry her to the waterfront."

Fong nodded and rushed to retrieve the items. Quickly he stashed them beneath his arms and hurried toward the river. Mr. Conroy smiled at Lee as he lifted her from the buggy.

"Your brother's excitement almost matches your gloom," Mr. Conroy commented when Fong motioned for them to hurry.

"Almost," Lee replied as she watched the junk gliding through the water toward shore, a huge-eyed, multicolored dragon painted on the bow. The four-cornered sails looked like giant venetian blinds, lowered and primed to catch the wind. "It's an ugly boat."

"I'm not very fond of dragons, myself," Mrs. Conroy agreed. The noises from the river grew louder as the music of bamboo flutes, zithers, and chimes floated through the air from the flower boats and mixed with the clanging gongs and chattering voices of the boatmen calling to each other. "Not a very quiet place, either!" she added.

Fong rushed back toward them. "I'll take her," he told Mr. Conroy. "I've already placed our belongings in the boat."

"Not yet!" Lee cried out, reaching toward Mrs. Conroy, who opened her arms to embrace her small, cherished friend one last time. Burrowing her head in Mrs. Conroy's shoulder, Lee inhaled deeply. She never wanted to forget the flower-garden smell or gentle smile of her friend. She wanted to remember it all in these last few minutes.

"You must go now, Lee," Mrs. Conroy softly told her.

"I know," she whispered.

"Do you have the name and address I gave you for Mrs. Mendelson?"

Yes, and I have yours, too," Lee replied proudly. "As soon as we get there, I'll write to you."

"And I promise that I'll write back. But you must remember that it takes a long time for letters to be delivered. Don't think I've forgotten you if my letter doesn't arrive as soon as you think it should."

"I won't," Lee replied with a halfhearted smile.

"Come," Fong stated sternly, once again reaching toward her.

"I'll walk," Lee answered defiantly.

"Let him carry you, Lee. When you arrive in Hong Kong, you may have to walk, and your feet will be sore. Then you'll regret your decision," Mrs. Conroy advised, giving her one last kiss.

Lee nodded and moved into her brother's arms.

"We'll be praying for you," Mrs. Conroy called after them as Fong trotted off toward the waiting boat.

Even when she could no longer make out the forms of Mr. and Mrs. Conroy on the riverbank, Lee continued to wave. She continued to wave until they were far, far from shore and she knew there was no turning back. They were going to America.

"I don't have enough room," Lee complained to her brother. "He keeps squishing me," she said, pointing to the man sitting beside her. "How long before we arrive in Hong Kong?"

"Early tomorrow morning, unless the breeze dies down. Now quit complaining—everybody is crowded," Fong answered, giving her no sympathy as he began singing along with some of the passengers. They were enjoying themselves, obviously happy to be floating toward Hong Kong. As the pale blue sky slowly turned into the gray shades of dusk, the men began making sacrifices to their Chinese gods. The man who was sprawled out beside Lee rose to toss a flaming paper into the water. Lee wasn't sure what their gods liked about flaming paper, but the glare as the blaze hit the sea cast an eerie glow. A glow that made the painted dragon on the bow of the junk appear even more evil than it had earlier. She shivered and huddled closer to her brother as the moon rose overhead.

"Try to sleep, and the time will pass more quickly," he said, cradling her head against his chest.

* * *

Lee rubbed her eyes and looked across the water. Squinting, she spied the looming outline of several buildings as they sailed through the thick fog into the harbor.

Finally, they reached the dock. "Come on," Fong urged as the other passengers began crawling up the makeshift wooden ladder to the dock.

"Wait. Let the others go first. My arms and legs are cramped from sitting so long—and from being squashed the whole time," she said, giving the man beside her a frown.

Lee watched as the men scrambled up to the dock. They were talking and laughing, jostling and pushing each other, acting like excited children on the first day of school. And, like her brother, they all seemed to be filled with the same desire to find gold in California. Gold fever! That's what Mrs. Conroy had called it.

During the night when Fong thought she was sleeping, he had talked with the other men about searching for gold and living in California. But Lee had been awake, carefully listening to her brother. She didn't care about the other men and their ambitions, but she wasn't sure about Fong's plans, which interested her deeply. Only once had she mentioned living in the city of Chinese people near San Francisco. He had listened to her, but promised nothing. Now she knew that living there was not in his plan—he was determined to search for gold. She would have to find some way to convince him during their voyage from Hong Kong to California.

"One of the men told me there is a dormitory where we can stay until our departure," Fong told her as he lifted her out of the junk.

"I'm not going to stay in a giant room with all those men," Lee protested. "I want to go and stay with the Mendelsons," she insisted.

"I don't know how to find them," he argued.

"Yung Lee! Yung Fong!" a loud voice called from just beyond the wooden dock. Both of them turned in unison and saw a large American man standing beside a horse and wagon. He was waving his arms wildly, motioning for them to come.

"Did you know they were meeting us?" Fong asked, a hint of anger in his voice.

"Mrs. Conroy said she had written to them. I wasn't sure," Lee meekly replied. "Why are you angry?"

"Because I want to remain here, close to the docks," he answered. "I don't want to go into the city."

"We must go and talk to him. It would be rude to ignore him after he has traveled to meet us," Lee insisted.

Fong grunted at her and grabbed their belongings. "Stay here. I'll go and talk to him."

"No! I want to come with you. Don't leave me here."

"I can't leave our belongings sitting alone. They will be stolen before we return. And I can't carry you and our belongings too."

"I can walk if you'll just be patient," she insisted.

"Fine. Walk!" he scowled as he picked up the baskets and suitcase that Mrs. Conroy had packed with Lee's belongings.

However, Lee couldn't possibly keep up, and he seemed to walk even more rapidly, just to prove his point. Suddenly she was swooped up into two big, strong arms that reminded her of Mr. Conroy.

"Let me carry you. I'm Harry Mendelson," the man told her. "And that's my wife, Ruth, standing by the wagon. The Conroys wrote us a letter and asked that we meet your junk. How would you like to stay with us until your ship departs for California?" he asked just as they caught up with Fong.

"I would like that very much," Lee replied before her

brother could say anything.

"We're going to stay in one of the dormitories," Fong said, ignoring his sister's answer.

"Have you seen the dormitories?" Mr. Mendelson inquired.

"Not yet, but one of the men who traveled with us from Canton told me they provide bunks and food. He said it doesn't cost much," Fong added.

"That much is true. But I don't think you'll want your sister sleeping there. I've never known of women staying in the dormitories. There are frequent fights, gambling, and other activities that wouldn't be suitable for a twelve-year-old girl," he advised.

Fong shifted from foot to foot. Lee could tell that Mr. Mendelson's words were making him uncomfortable. It wouldn't look good if he insisted that she go with him after being warned of the living conditions. Yet Lee knew that he didn't want to give in and let her go with the Mendelsons.

"You can stay in the dormitory, and I'll go with the Mendelsons," Lee ventured. "I promise to be here before the ship sails. Just tell us when we need to be here."

"I've already checked with the captain of the Flying Cloud. The ship sails in three days at daybreak. I will have Lee here to meet you if you'd rather not stay with us," Mr. Mendelson confirmed. "But you are also welcome in our home, Fong. I'm sure you would find it more comfortable."

Fong looked surprised at Mr. Mendelson's remarks. "How did you know we would be sailing on the *Flying Cloud*?"

"Mrs. Conroy mentioned it in her letter."

"Of course. I should have known," he said. "My sister will give me no peace if I insist upon her staying here. She can go with you, and I'll stay here, close to the docks."

"Thank you, Fong!" Lee said, delighted with his choice.

"Make sure you are not late, Lee. Our future depends upon it."

"I promise," she happily answered, waving good-bye as

Mr. Mendelson placed her in the buggy beside his wife.

"Mrs. Conroy said to send you her greetings. And I want to thank you for coming to get me," Lee said, giving Mrs. Mendelson her biggest smile.

"It's our pleasure. We haven't had a young girl around for a long time."

"Did you live in Boston too?" Lee asked Mrs. Mendelson shortly after they arrived at the house.

"No, I grew up in San Francisco. My father was a banker, and a friend encouraged him to move west when I was very young. I don't remember any other home. Except for here in Hong Kong, of course," she quickly added. "Why don't you sit here beside me on the sofa?" Mrs. Mendelson said, patting the cushion beside her.

"San Francisco?" Lee's eyes sparkled with excitement as she sat down.

"Yes, the very same city you're going to," Mrs. Mendelson replied.

"I have lots of questions for you," Lee said, scooting closer to her new friend, "about a town that looks like China. I think it's somewhere close to San Francisco. Do you know about it?"

"Of course. It's called Chinatown. What do you want to know?"

Lee was dumbfounded. There really was a town of Chinese people in California. If she could find out about this place, maybe, just maybe, she could persuade Fong to forget about searching for gold.

"Have you ever been to this Chinatown?" Lee asked, trying to hide her excitement.

"Oh, yes, several times. We have a friend who lives just outside the borders of Chinatown. She oversees a small mission and a school for Chinese children," Mrs. Mendelson explained.

"What is it like?" Lee asked, edging even closer to the older woman.

"It's a large house. They've made the first floor into class-rooms where the children learn English, and there are several Chinese girls who live there all the time with Mrs. Wilson. Two other ladies from the Presbyterian church come and help teach lessons," Mrs. Mendelson explained.

"No, that's not what I wanted to know," Lee replied. "I want to know what Chinatown looks like."

"Oh, what Chinatown looks like. Well, let me see if I can explain it. Chinatown will remind you of Canton, only it is much, much smaller with fewer people, and most of them are men. There are shops that sell food and spices as well as other Chinese goods, and everyone speaks in Chinese. It's not the same as being in China, but the next best thing, I suppose," Mrs. Mendelson stated.

"Perhaps like being an American and living in the European sector of Canton?" Lee ventured.

"Yes. That's a very good comparison," Mrs. Mendelson praised. "Why all this interest in Chinatown? I thought your brother was sailing to America in search of gold."

"He is. But if I must move to America, I think I would rather live in Chinatown," Lee answered.

"Well, I don't think that your brother will discover any gold in Chinatown. Unless he changes his mind and decides to open a business for himself or go to work for one of the other businessmen, I wouldn't plan on living there," Mrs. Mendelson warned.

"I'm hoping he will change his mind," Lee replied with a sheepish grin.

"I wouldn't count on that. Once people get gold fever, there seems to be no turning back until they either find gold or no longer have the money to continue searching."

"Once he sees Chinatown, he may decide it's best to remain there," Lee confidently answered.

Living in California might not be so bad after all. I know I can convince Fong, she decided as Mrs. Mendelson tucked her into bed that night. When sleep didn't come, her confidence weakened and Mrs. Mendelson's warning marched in and out of her dreams throughout the night.

Chapter Three

HONG KONG

"Where are the other passengers?" Lee asked her brother. "There should be more people if we are to sail in thirty minutes!"

"I know, I know! I'm thinking," Fong snapped.

"Well, you'd better think quickly. Mr. Mendelson has already departed, and I don't want to stay here!"

"Quit heckling me. Stay here while I find someone to ask. And don't move!"

A few moments later, Fong came racing back toward her. "*The Flying Cloud* is not sea-worthy, and they've transferred all passengers and cargo to another ship—the *Senator*. It's berthed on the other end of the docks," he panted, pointing toward some distant spot on the foggy horizon.

His chest was heaving up and down, like bellows fanning a flame into fire. "We have only a short time to get over there, and I can't carry both you and the baggage. Let's go," he shouted as he filled his arms with their belongings and bolted away from her, speeding down the wooden dock.

"Hurry! They'll sail without us," Fong called urgently over his shoulder. His queue of braided hair was hanging down his back and swayed from side to side as he scurried toward the waiting vessel.

"I can't. You go on. I'll be there as soon as I can," Lee cried.

"I'll take our belongings to the ship and be back for you," he promised, breaking into a full sprint.

Lingering for a moment, she watched him run. His agile gait was a painful reminder of her awkward stride. Hobbling along on her tiny bound feet, she finally reached the dock from which they would sail. Slowly she moved among the stacks of cargo waiting to be loaded onto the ship.

Her eyes widened at the sight. Swarming on the dock were hundreds of Chinese men wearing loose shirts and trousers, their heads covered with pointy straw hats. Most of them balanced long poles across their shoulders, with a bamboo basket attached to each end. As they turned and swayed about, the poles began swinging back and forth like the spokes of a giant Ferris wheel going around and around and around.

Fong returned to where she stood waiting just as a thunderous bell began to clang. The moment the dreadful bonging ceased, the ship's captain came to the top of the gangplank. Holding a shiny, trumpet-shaped object to his mouth, he began shouting orders.

"I've never seen one of those. I can't believe how easily we can hear every word he says when we are standing so far away," Fong remarked.

"It is surprising!" Lee agreed. "But I don't think many of the passengers understood him. I think he needs to speak in Chinese."

Lee decided that the captain must have had the same thought when he gave the horn to a Chinese man standing on deck. Instantly, the waiting passengers began forming two lines. They trudged up the gangplank toward the captain, side by side, one after another, resembling the double column of animals that marched onto the ark to meet Noah.

"The gangplank is steep and much too difficult for you to climb," Fong stated.

"I want to walk!"

"Don't argue with me, Lee," he warned, lifting her into his arms. "Didn't you hear the captain? I don't think he is a patient man."

Turning away so that Fong couldn't see the tears beginning to spill down her cheeks, Lee stopped squirming as he carried her aboard. The two of them stood near the railing, staring at the multitude of shabby buildings scattered along the wharf. For three months she had argued with Fong that they should remain in China. For three months he had resisted. Now there was no time left for argument.

She wanted to scream at the sailors to refasten the thick hemp ropes to the dock and push the wobbly gangplank back into place. But she knew nobody would listen. The only hope that remained was to convince Fong to settle in Chinatown. *Maybe, just maybe*, she thought.

"It won't be so terrible. As soon as we've found gold, we can return to China, if you want," her brother promised once again as the ship sliced through the murky green water and out into the South China Sea.

"You mean *if* we find gold, don't you?"

"We'll find gold. It's everywhere in California! Once you've seen the streets of gold, I don't think you will want to leave."

"Mrs. Conroy says the only streets paved with gold are in heaven. And I will want to return to my China," she quietly replied while leaning over the rail to watch the white foamy caps of water curling along the side of the ship.

"What's so wonderful about staying in China? We lost our whole family to the war between the provinces. At least the Americans don't fight among themselves," he declared.

"How do you know? All you know is what you've heard from sailors. They don't live in California. They don't live anywhere. Sailing from port to port, they spin their tales of gold and a better life. If there is so much gold in California, why do they still work on these ships? Mrs. Conroy says . . ."

"You talk too much! If you ever want to make a good marriage, you'd better learn not to question everything a man tells you."

"I don't talk too much, and I don't care if I ever get married. You always say that when you can't answer my questions."

Lee turned to see two dirty, dark-bearded sailors pointing

and laughing at her feet as they approached the railing where she and Fong stood.

"Look at them feet. Her mama must have hated her!" one of the sailors said to the other.

"Can you imagine bouncing around on them things? It'd be like walking on your tippy-toes all the time," he said, lifting himself up on his toes and taking tiny steps while his friend doubled over in laughter.

"I heard tell they wrapped up little girls' feet like that to make 'em small, but I never did believe it. Bunch of barbarians, if you ask me!"

"What can you expect? They're all a pack of heathens that worship idols. It's probably one of those rituals they do—you know, like a sacrifice or something."

"Come on. We need to go below," Fong said, motioning for her to say nothing to the sailors. "I'm sorry you had to hear that. They don't know what they're talking about, so just ignore them."

"Don't you care that they made fun of me or called us names? Is that what the Americans think of Chinese?"

"How do I know what they think? Besides, it doesn't matter. Once we've found gold, we can live wherever we want," he said, turning his back to her and moving toward the stairs.

Clinging to the makeshift rope railing, she followed her brother down the dark stairway into their living quarters— quarters they would share with the hundreds of other Chinese emigrants she had watched march onto the ship.

Waiting a few moments for her eyes to adjust to the semi-darkness, Lee slowly entered the room. She blinked several times, but the bleak sight didn't go away. Row upon row of bunkbeds filled the huge area, giving it a prison-like appearance. The passengers were sitting or lying on top of the bunks they had claimed. Bamboo baskets filled with their clothing, bedrolls, and other personal belongings rested on the wooden floor beside them.

"Is this where we are expected to live? We'll be crammed in this room tighter than silkworms on a tray! Did you know it would be like this?" she asked, giving him an accusing stare.

"Keep your voice down and remain calm," her brother cautioned. "Just because I allow you to talk to me as an equal doesn't mean that our fellow countrymen will understand. We'll be fine. You'll see."

*   *   *

Lee reminded her brother of those words when raging storms and winds roared around them several days later as they were nearing the Philippine Islands. Hour after hour, day after day, the massive ship continued to rise on the crest of the waves and then plunge itself downward, as if urgently seeking the bottom of the ocean.

"I can't stand this any longer," Lee whispered to her brother as he attempted to comfort her. "My stomach churns constantly; it's so hot I can hardly breathe; and when I do, it stinks! I feel as though I'm sitting in the middle of a garbage heap during the hottest day of summer. Can't someone force the captain to open the hatch?"

"No. If a huge wave comes over the side of the ship, it will spill down the stairway, and we'll be flooded and drown."

"Cool water running down into this awful place sounds wonderful to me. If I could scrub away some of this smelly mess, I'd be willing to take my chances on drowning," she complained in a weak voice.

"I think you would change your mind if the water covered your head and you couldn't breathe. Come on now, eat some of this food. You need to remain strong," he encouraged her.

"Eat? You think I should eat that slop they are serving us?"

"It will give you strength, even if it does taste foul," he said.

"I think I would rather die! I wonder what our parents would think if they were alive."

"Well, they aren't alive, and we're on this ship. There's nothing I can do about it now, so quit trying to make me feel guilty," he retorted.

"If you had listened to me, we wouldn't be in this predicament! But, no, you wouldn't hear a thing I said. After all, I'm a girl and girls can't possibly make an intelligent decision. Well, if I were making the choices, we wouldn't be eating that horrid bean paste soup and pickled radish. We wouldn't be drinking that terrible brew made from seawater that they call tea. And that rice they give us—it's so hard I can't even swallow it. If I were making the choices, we wouldn't be served our meals from a bucket like a bunch of farm animals, and . . ."

"That's enough, Lee. I know you didn't want to leave China. You've made that very clear. But the fact is that we will survive this journey. I know it. And once we get to California, everything is going to be fine. You'll see."

"That's what you told me our first day at sea. But everything isn't fine; everything is dreadful!"

* * *

Two days later when the waters had calmed, a scraggly looking sailor came below and ordered the passengers up on deck—all except for ten of the men who appeared the strongest. They remained below and were ordered to clean the area.

"Why must Chinese passengers clean it? That should be the sailors' duty," Lee whispered to her brother.

"Probably because they didn't have enough money for passage. I talked to some of them while I was staying at the dormitory in Hong Kong. They agreed to work in return for their passage," he explained.

"For how long?" Lee asked.

"Most of them told me for two years," he replied.

"That is foolish! Why don't they save their money and then travel to America? Their lives in the United States will be worse than in China," she predicted.

"You don't know that. Once they've worked off their debt, they can begin their new lives."

"They want to be rich but are unwilling to wait until they can afford to buy a ticket. What good is it to get to a new country if your life belongs to another? At least you didn't do that. Did you?" she asked.

"No," he quickly answered. "I used the small inheritance from our parents and some of the money I saved while working in Canton. We'll be free to live wherever we want."

Two scruffy looking sailors moved alongside the ship's railing near where they stood. The man closest to Lee gave them a look filled with hatred. "If we keep hauling all these Chinee into Californey, there'll soon be more of them than us."

"If they was smart, they'd stay in China—ain't nobody wants their kind moving in. But they'll find that out soon enough," the other sailor replied with an evil laugh.

"Guess they must be as stupid as everyone says," his friend agreed, joining in the laughter.

Lee turned and began to say something, but Fong quickly whispered for her to keep quiet.

"Look! There's that little misfit with the puny feet," the first sailor said. "I'd like to see her run—that would be a good laugh."

"Hey—you two sailors—get back to work. This ain't no pleasure trip," the first mate yelled at the men, who quickly moved away.

Lee spun toward her brother as soon as the men were out of earshot. "Why won't you let me talk?"

"It would only cause trouble. Besides, we learn more if they don't think we can understand their language."

"That's certainly true. What we've learned is that the Americans don't like Chinese. They think we are all barbarians and heathen idol worshipers—that we are stupid. What's more, I'm sure we'll find out that the Americans will be telling us where we can live. You may find that the gold you're looking for isn't for the Chinese!"

"I know better. I've talked to men who have already been

to California and struck gold. They said that the Americans didn't like them very well, but if they kept quiet and went about their business, everything was fine."

"What? You mean you want to live among people who think we are ignorant heathens just so you can become rich?"

"I didn't say I want to. But if it is necessary, I'm willing."

"Mrs. Mendelson told me about a place called Chinatown. She visited there before moving to Hong Kong. It's near San Francisco, and she said the Chinese people appeared very happy. She told me there are many streets lined with Chinese businesses, just like in our homeland. Nobody bothers the Chinese people living there or calls them nasty names. If we must live in California, I think we should live there," Lee told him.

"You don't find gold living in a town filled with Chinese people," Fong scornfully replied.

But before Lee could say anything further, the passengers who were standing alongside them on the ship's deck began to shout and celebrate.

"Look!" Fong cried, his voice filled with excitement as he pointed toward the horizon. "We've arrived! It's Dai Fou, the big city."

Chapter Four

SAN FRANCISCO

As the ship sliced through the water toward their final destination, Lee stood squashed among the other passengers. They were packed together more tightly than sardines in a can. She could barely breathe, and the cloudless blue sky that had been a delight only moments earlier was now blotted out by the straw hats of the men towering over her. Just when she thought she could bear it no longer, the ship entered its berth, and they received permission to leave the ship. In a slow, methodical procession, the passengers began snaking their way down the gangplank and into a run-down building at one end of the dock. A weatherworn sign swinging over the door announced that they were entering the Pacific Mail Steamship Company. Lee blinked several times as they walked into the building. The semidarkness that shrouded the room made it difficult for her to see.

"This place is as bad as the ship—maybe worse," Lee whispered to her brother as she continued to survey their surroundings.

"Get in line and shut your traps," one of the officials hollered at the men who were pushing their way into the building. He used a long wooden club to poke them first in one direction and then another.

"Why is he being so mean?" Lee asked. "All we want to do is be on our way. Why don't they just let us pass through?"

"I don't know. But we need to do as we're told," Fong replied while shifting her to his other arm.

"What have we got here?" the official asked, using his club to turn Lee's face toward him. "Looks like we got us a little slant-eyed girl among all these ugly men. She yours?" he asked Fong while motioning from Fong to Lee.

Fong nodded, but said nothing.

"I bet I could get a good price for this little gal, what with the shortage of Chinese women around these parts," the man called out to several other inspectors sitting at a rickety wooden table in the center of the room. Loud guffaws and snickers of agreement burst forth from the group. One of the guards was laughing so hard that he began to choke on the wad of tobacco tucked into his cheek.

"Serves him right," Lee commented as the man gasped for air. Finally catching his breath, Lee watched the man shoot a brown stream of saliva into a metal spittoon sitting nearby. "He's disgusting!"

"Keep your voice down! We don't need any trouble," Fong warned.

"Women and girls go to the other side of the room," the guard instructed Fong. He pointed toward a doorway that separated the two rooms and then motioned toward Lee.

Fong looked from the doorway back toward the official and acted as though he didn't understand. "Get over here," the official called out to a stoop-shouldered Chinese interpreter. "Tell him this girl must go to the other section," he repeated to the Chinaman.

Lee shook her head when the man finished giving them the instructions. "I must stay with my brother," she insisted, speaking in her native language.

"Does she understand?" the guard asked the interpreter. "She understand," the Chinaman answered as he walked away. "She not want to leave her brother, but she understand," he repeated.

"She ain't leaving him—she's just going to the women's quarters," the official replied, pulling Lee from her brother's arms.

"Quit struggling. You're only making things harder on both

of us," Fong whispered as he released her to the guard.

"How long must I stay there?" Lee called out to the interpreter, who was now standing across the room.

"Two, maybe three days," he answered, holding up three fingers.

Fear washed over Lee as the guard deposited her in the unsightly room. It was big enough for at least fifteen cots, but there were none. A chamber pot and crude wooden bench were the only furnishings. Instead of a sunlit bedroom adorned with wallpaper and carpet, the walls and floor were constructed of nothing more than splintered wooden planks. There were no lovely paintings in ornate frames or soft music floating through the air from Mrs. Conroy's piano. Soft melodic tunes had been replaced by shrieking gulls and clamoring men in the next room. Hobbling over to the bench along the south wall, she hunched down and stared at the floor. Now what? If only there were someone to talk to—at least Fong had the other men to keep him company. She had no one. Unlike her brother, all of the other Chinese men left their wives and daughters at home when they went off in search of gold. Those men dreamed of becoming rich and returning to their homeland. But not Fong! He had to drag her along to this horrid, smelly place. She shuddered at the sound of an approaching guard, but gave a sigh of relief when he continued past the door. She would much rather be alone than have one of those bad-tempered guards coming around making rude remarks.

"Thank you, Jesus," she uttered, relief wrapping around her like a warm blanket. Jesus! Why hadn't she thought about Him before now? Mrs. Conroy had reminded her that she would always have a friend with her. If she ever needed a friend, it was now. "I'm sorry I forgot about You," Lee spoke aloud. "But I'm glad You never forget about me. I guess You know what's going on down here. These guards are not very nice—they remind me of the guards that were so mean to the

Apostle Paul. Maybe You could cause an earthquake so we can get out of here, just like You did for Paul back in Jerusalem. Do You think that might work?" she questioned aloud.

"Who you talking to, girl?" a burly guard with a jagged scar on his face questioned from the doorway.

Since Fong thought it better that no one knew they spoke English, she continued to pretend she didn't understand. She gazed down at the floor and hoped the guard would return to the men in the other room.

"I asked who you was talking to," the man repeated, walking toward her. Lee observed the pair of scuffed brown boots that were directly in front of her. Her eyes flitted back and forth between her tiny bound feet and the enormous boot-clad feet of the guard.

"Cat got your tongue?" he finally questioned, breaking the silence between them.

"What cat?" she asked, forgetting herself.

"Ah-ha! So you can understand English," the guard replied, seating himself beside her on the bench. He took one large finger, placed it under her chin, and gently turned her face toward him. "I'm not going to hurt you, missy. This is one terrible place for a young girl on her own. You're gonna have to trust someone eventually—it might as well be me."

"Why should I trust you?" Lee asked doubtfully.

"'Cause far as I can tell, you ain't got many other choices. 'Sides, I'm a pretty good guy to trust. My name's Charlie Landers. What's yours?" he asked, giving her a little chuckle.

"My name is Yung Lee, but I'm not alone. I've got my brother, Yung Fong. He's over there," she said, pointing toward the wall that separated the rooms. "And why are you a good person to trust?" she asked, mustering up her courage.

"We-l-l-l," he drawled, "just between you and me, I got a friend named Jesus, and I thought I heard you talking to Him. You know—when I was standing outside the doorway." He hesitated for a moment. "Were you talkin' to my Jesus?" he asked.

Lee thought she could see a sparkle in his eyes—and he didn't look quite so mean as she had earlier thought. "Yes, I was talking to Jesus," she meekly answered.

"Well, don't that just beat all. You, a little Chinese girl, and me, a big American man, having the same friend. "How did you meet my friend Jesus?" he asked, giving her an encouraging smile that revealed snaggly front teeth.

"I lived with American missionaries in Canton, Mr. and Mrs. Conroy. Perhaps you know them?" she asked.

"Nope, 'fraid not. I don't go to sea anymore—had my fill of that years ago. In fact, I've only been in Californey a couple of years. Came out here lookin' for gold," he explained.

"Did you ever find any?" she inquired.

"Naw, never did find any of that, but I did find Jesus. And that's more wonderful than any gold this earth's got to offer, ain't it?"

Lee nodded her head in agreement. "My brother thinks the streets are paved with gold in America, but Mrs. Conroy said the only streets lined with gold are in heaven. She showed me in the Bible—in the Book of Revelation," Lee added.

"I ain't read that book yet. I'm kind of a slow reader. But Pastor Roten done explained to me all about how to get to heaven and how Jesus died for me. It was hard for me to believe that at first—you know what with me being a scraggly old sailor who has been in and out of trouble all his life. But he told me Jesus died for everyone—even for the likes of me."

Lee gave him a reassuring smile. "Mrs. Conroy said the same thing. She said that all you have to do is invite Jesus to come into your heart and ask Him to forgive your sins. And there He is, waiting to welcome you with open arms."

"It's hard for an old salt like me to believe it can be so simple—I keep thinking I've got to do more. But me and my friend Jesus have been together for nearly a year now, and He's been takin' good care of me and ain't asked for nothin' else," he confided.

"Except sometimes it's hard to do what's right, especially when people treat you badly," Lee commented.

"That's true enough. The Good Book says to turn the other cheek, but it's not always easy."

"Do any of the other guards know Jesus?" Lee ventured. "They don't seem very nice."

"I don't think so, but I just started working here a few weeks ago. It's not a very friendly place."

"Landers! What are you doing in there? Get off your duff and get busy," one of the officials yelled from the doorway.

"I'll be back later. Keep talkin' to Jesus, and maybe between the two of us we can find a way to get you out of here," Landers whispered as he rose from the bench and left the room.

"Oh, thank you, Jesus," Lee whispered, grateful for her new friend. "You sent someone to help us! If He can get us out of this awful place, things will be much better. That isn't too much to ask all in one day, is it? I know You can help."

As the minutes ticked by into hours, Lee grew restless and began doubting the guard's promise to return. "Maybe God has another plan to help me. I guess the best thing to do right now is fix a place to sleep," she murmured.

Climbing down from the bench, she gathered together some of the dirty straw that was scattered about the room. The wooden floor bounced with each step she took. What if it caved in and she dropped into the water? The ocean would surely swallow her up in one giant gulp. But then perhaps it would spit her back out on the docks at Canton, and that would be a welcome event. She laughed aloud at her silliness, and quickly finished piling the straw into a makeshift bed. It wouldn't be like sleeping on Mrs. Conroy's goose-down mattress, but at least it would make the floor a bit softer. She had just lain down when the guard named Landers entered the room carrying a bowl of food.

"You've been gone so long, I thought you weren't going to

come back," Lee said as he approached her.

"My boss has been watching me. He just went home to eat his supper, so I thought I could sneak in for a few minutes. Here, eat this," he said, shoving the bowl toward her.

Lee gobbled down the rice, wishing there had been more in the bowl. "That's the best rice I've had since we left China," she said, smacking her lips.

"I'm sorry there wasn't more. Only one scoop per bowl. That's the rule. I managed to get you two scoops without being caught," he said with a wide grin.

"Have you planned how we can escape from here?" Lee asked. "Did you talk to my brother and tell him that I'm all right?"

"I haven't come up with a plan just yet. I talked to your brother, and he thinks it might be best to wait and go through the entry process with everyone else. He doesn't want to risk being caught. He's probably right," Landers confidently replied.

"What? You agree with him that we should stay in this awful place?" Lee asked, horrified by Landers' agreement with her brother.

"Well, to be honest, you're a sight more comfortable than all those men crammed into that little space next door. None of them has a pile of straw to rest upon, or a speck of privacy, for that matter. Besides, you may be released as early as tomorrow, and I'll help you find your way into Chinatown then," he replied. "I best be getting back over there before I'm missed. You say your prayers and try to get some sleep," he added, waving his huge hand in farewell.

Quickly rearranging her position, Lee lay down on the straw mattress and tightly closed her eyes. "I thought You were going to help me escape," she said accusingly into the darkness. "Why did You send Landers if he's not going to help us get out of this place? I don't need a friend to talk to. I already have You. I don't like being in this new country, and I hope that Fong is just as cold as I am. Oh, yes, thanks for the straw," she said. "Amen!" she emphatically added—just in case God didn't know how genuinely unhappy she was.

A short time later, Lee slipped into a fitful sleep, tossing and turning as scenes of the Conroys and her life in Canton paraded through her dreams. Voices of the awakening men in the next room startled Lee from sleep early the next morning. She rolled over on the straw, glancing upward toward where the ceiling should have been. But instead, there were only wooden beams covered by sagging shingles which were flapping up and down in the breeze. Birds had found their way through missing shingles and were hard at work building nests above her head. A glowing morning sun began to peek over the horizon, casting narrow shafts of golden light between the cracks of the boarded walls. It took a few moments before realization set in—the realization that she was far from the security of the Conroys' home in China.

"I see you made it through the night," Landers said, bringing her a bowl of lukewarm porridge.

"Ugh," she remarked, holding the spoon in mid-air while he observed the porridge hanging from her utensil like a giant glob of paste. "You can take this back. I don't think it's really food."

"You better try to eat it. You won't get anything else until tonight. They don't serve anything for lunch. It's just breakfast and supper around this place."

"If you can call it that," Lee replied, taking a small bite of the gruel and making a face.

"I think I've convinced my boss to let you and your brother leave by tomorrow morning," Landers said, in a voice brimming with pride.

"I was hoping for this morning," Lee replied. Seeing the hurt look that crossed Landers' face, she quickly apologized. "I'm sorry to be so ungrateful, mister. I know you're doing everything you can to help us. Thank you for your trouble."

He gave her one of his wide grins. "You're welcome, missy. Your brother said to bid you good morning, and he sent this blanket in case you need it tonight. I need to get going before I get in trouble. That wouldn't help any of us," he added.

Lee's gaze rested on the doorway long after Landers left the room. Mrs. Conroy was right. What was it that the older woman had said just a few days before Lee's departure for America? That everyone is special and looks exactly the way God intended? Yes—that was it! We are all perfect in God's sight. Well, Charlie Landers was certainly a good example of that teaching. A picture of the burly sailor flashed through her mind. If Lee lined up all the people she had seen throughout the journey and since her arrival in San Francisco, she would have never picked Charlie Landers as the person God would send to help. It made her smile. *Sometimes God does use the most unlikely people to teach us lessons*, she thought.

The day crawled along at a snail's pace. Lee longed for a window that would permit a view of the ships sailing in and out of the harbor. The cracks between the wooden slats of the building provided her with the muted voices of sailors and the smell of fishy saltwater, but they were no substitute for a window. In due time, the incessant boredom caused her to rearrange the straw bedding several times while a spider, busily spinning its web in a nearby corner, momentarily held her interest. What would Mrs. Conroy do in this place? Without her Bible to read, she would probably recite memory verses or sing hymns, Lee decided. And so she began, one after another, reciting all the scripture verses that Mrs. Conroy had helped her commit to memory.

Landers appeared at the door as the sun was beginning its slow descent beyond the horizon for another day. "Are you ready to get out of this place?" he asked.

"Oh, yes!" Lee answered clapping her hands. "Do you mean it? Can we really leave?"

"Yes. Your brother has already left and is waiting on the

dock," he said. Leaning down, he lifted her into his brawny arms and hoisted her high in the air. He was a giant of a man, and Lee was glad for his protection.

The other guards merely nodded at Landers as he carried Lee from the room and continued out of the building. The two of them soon noticed Fong standing near a stack of cargo on the dock, and Lee began waving both arms.

"It's good to see you. Isn't Landers wonderful? He knows Jesus, too," Lee said as they approached her brother.

"Yes, he is a very nice man, and I appreciate his help," Fong replied, his tone formal.

"Fong doesn't know Jesus," Lee informed her new friend.

"Landers doesn't care whether I am a Christian or not," Fong abruptly retorted.

"Of course, I care," Landers countered. "Knowing Jesus is the most important thing in life. You need to listen to your sister and discover the wonders of our faith," he stated, giving Fong a genial slap on the back.

"Are you going to show us the direction to Chinatown?" Fong asked, skillfully turning the conversation away from the subject of Jesus.

"We're on our way," Landers replied, taking long strides across the street. "Let me carry some of your bags," he offered, grabbing one of the bags as they headed up the street.

Landers pointed out some of the local businesses as they proceeded down the street. "See that ship over there? The one that's been pulled up between those other buildings?"

"Why is there a ship sitting on land?" Lee asked, clearly perplexed by the sight.

"There's more than one," Landers explained, pointing up the street to several other ships. "These were ships that carried passengers and cargo and sailed the high seas at one time. When their crews deserted them and went off in search of gold, the ship owners didn't have much choice. They could let their boats rot out there in the water, or they could use a little ingenuity. The fellers that owned these ships decided to tow them ashore and use them as ready-made businesses. That one there's a general store, and the one down there," he said, pointing at a bright red and yellow boat, "is a saloon."

"They surely make a curious sight," Lee commented as she observed the ships nestled among the other wooden buildings. "But probably not any more curious than the three of us!" They had been receiving their share of gawking stares—the huge scarred seaman carrying a Chinese girl, and a Chinese man running alongside them, loaded down with baggage.

"Well, here it is," Landers told them after they had been walking for half an hour. "This here is the beginnings of the Chinese part of town. Guess we'd better part company, 'cause I don't know much about Chinatown. Besides, you'll probably get more help without the likes of me along," he explained.

"Will we ever see you again?" Lee asked, not wanting to say good-bye.

"You never know. If not in this life, then in the next," he promised while giving her a wink.

She smiled and gave him a hug. "Thank you for being my friend and helping us," she whispered.

"My pleasure," he replied, turning away and giving her a final wave of his arm.

"Come on!" Fong ordered when she stood staring after Landers. "We need to find a place to spend the night before it gets too dark."

"You didn't even thank Mr. Landers. He was kind and helped us, but you're in such a hurry that you must have thought it would take too much time to be courteous. Sometimes I don't understand you," Lee criticized.

"He knew I was grateful for his help. Besides, he's probably just as anxious to get back home as I am to find a room for us to stay tonight. Now, hurry up," Fong snapped back at her.

"I'm coming, but you don't have to be so crabby!" Lee responded.

"You just do as you're told, and everything will be fine. I'm tired and want to find a place to sleep before it gets dark. Is that asking so much?"

"You shouldn't be worried about it getting dark. I'm sure that the moon shining on all these streets of gold will make it bright enough for you to see all night long," Lee said with a giggle.

Fong's look was enough to stop her laughter—at least outwardly. Inside, she was having a good belly laugh at her brother's obvious disappointment that the streets were made of dirt and wood, not the shiny gold that had lured him to America.

Chapter Five

CHINATOWN

Fong came to an abrupt halt in front of a Chinese apothecary shop at the corner of Dupont and Clay streets. A red and gold sign advertising furnished rooms for rent above the store caused them to stop and then enter. Lee remained as silent as a church mouse while Fong questioned the shop owner about the cost. Moments later, the two were bantering back and forth, with frowns etched upon their faces and arms gesturing wildly. Finally, they agreed upon a price that seemed to satisfy both of them. Digging into one of the baskets, Fong pulled out several coins and placed them in the owner's hand, whose fingers snapped tightly over the coins as he beckoned them to follow along behind him. Scurrying through the shop, he directed them toward a narrow stairway and then pointed upward.

"Up the steps to the end of the hall. Last door," he instructed, then turned and hurried back toward the front of his store.

The tiny room had space enough only for two cots and a washstand, but it was clean and they felt safe. Lee sat down on the cot and gave a squeal of delight. The bed was small, but the mattress was soft and the sheets were fresh. She slipped into a deep sleep only moments after pulling the covers under her chin. The next morning, the sound of customers in the shop below finally awakened her.

"Hurry up," Fong urged. "We need to get some directions and be on our way."

"We have the rest of our lives, Fong. I don't know why you're in such a rush," Lee replied as she carefully folded her belongings and returned them to one of the baskets.

"Because I want to begin searching for gold. I didn't come to Gam Saan so that I could sleep—I came to find gold."

"Well, I haven't seen any golden streets, and I certainly haven't seen any gold mountains. What's more, I don't think we will," Lee replied. "Why don't we just stay here in Chinatown? I'm sure we can find a way to earn money and support ourselves. Please, Fong, won't you at least think about it?"

"No! I came here to find gold, and that's what I intend to do," he stubbornly answered as he carried her down the stairway and into the pharmacy. "Stay here until I retrieve our things," he ordered, racing back upstairs to gather their belongings.

"How did you sleep?" the shop owner inquired as Fong placed the last of their baggage on the floor.

"We slept well, thank you. As you know, I am new to Gam Saan and in need of some help. Can you direct me to a member of the Kong Chow Association? I am from Kwangtung province," he added.

The man nodded. "You need to meet with Sam Yee. His business is across the street—there, that one," he said pointing toward a shop that advertised a variety of hardware and household products for sale. "You may leave your baggage here while you go to visit him, if you wish," the pharmacist offered.

"Thank you," Fong replied as he scooped Lee into his arms and raced across the street, his waist-long, braided queue slapping back and forth as he ran.

"I'm looking for Sam Yee," Fong told an older gentleman who approached them as they walked inside the store.

"I am Sam Yee. How may I help?"

"I was told that the Kong Chow Association would help me with proper provisions for gold mining when I reached Gam Saan. I have money to pay for the necessary goods, but I need advice on what items I need to purchase and where I will find gold," Fong stated.

The man's eyes twinkled; then he laughed. "I can help you with the provisions, and I can give you advice on how to search for gold. But I'm afraid I can't tell you where to find it. If I knew, I'd go and get it myself."

Fong smiled back at the man. "If you can just tell me the general direction, that would be helpful."

"People leave San Francisco going all directions in search of gold. If I were going, I would probably head north up the Sacramento River. There is a small Chinese settlement up that way if you would prefer to live among our fellow country-men. Come, I'll show you the supplies you will need," Mr. Yee said, leading Fong toward shelves stocked with an array of picks, axes, shovels, and food supplies.

Moving aside a stack of fabric, Lee wiggled onto an ornate iron bench. She watched as her brother scampered about the store while assembling piles of tools, food, and household supplies. Growing weary of Fong's frantic shopping spree, Lee scooted off the bench and tottered outside. She took a deep whiff of the spring air; it smelled like home. This town reminded her of Canton, only much smaller. A man passed by carrying baskets filled with live chickens that he was taking to market, and there were peddlers sitting on street corners hawking their wares. Four little boys marched down the street, holding onto each other's queues and forming a pigtail parade. They looked like circus elephants linking their tails and trunks. The sight made her giggle.

A few moments later, Fong's demanding voice interrupted her reverie. "Let's go get our baggage. Mr. Yee has arranged for a wagon to take us to the river where we will board a boat."

"So soon? Why can't we stay here for a while?" Lee begged, longing to remain in this place that made her feel as if she were home.

"There is no reason to remain here. I've come to find gold, and I want to begin as soon as possible. I've already explained this," her brother replied, his voice growing impatient as they returned to the apothecary shop. Fong placed her beside their baggage before purchasing some herbs and medical supplies from the pharmacist.

Out on the street again, Fong shouted, "There! There's our wagon. Over here!" he cried out to the driver while frantically waving his arms. "Come on, Lee. He's coming," her brother yelled.

The driver pulled on the reins, and the horses came to a halt in front of the pharmacy. Fong raced back and forth, first loading their baggage and supplies and then carrying Lee and placing her in the rear of the wagon. Finally, he jumped onto the seat, leaned back, and drew a deep breath. "We're ready," he told the man, who merely nodded, released the brake, and slapped the reins, which encouraged the horses to move forward.

Lee bounced along in the back of the wagon, the rutted paths leading toward the river tossing her first one direction and then another. She finally wedged herself between two large gunnysacks containing rice. It helped some, but her stomach seemed to flip over at least three times during the short journey.

"This is it. The boat should be along any time now. Those people are probably waiting for it too," the driver told Fong as he helped unload their supplies beside the riverbank.

Lee glanced toward the group of people standing a short distance away. Since all of them had dark skin and black, wiry hair, she decided they must be a family. She had never seen black people before, and she hoped Fong would let her visit with them.

"You going to the gold fields?" the man called out to Fong. Fong nodded. "You?"

"Oh, I already got a claim. We just come into San Francisco to celebrate and give the missus a chance to do some shopping. We live up near Striker's Gulch. Where you headed?" he asked while moving closer.

"We're heading north, but I'm not sure how far—haven't decided," Fong replied as Lee continued watching the family.

"I'm Silas Smith. This here's my wife, Mary, and these are my younguns, John, Lizzy, and Ben," he said, pointing toward each of the children as he recited their names.

"I am Yung Fong, and this is my sister, Yung Lee," Fong replied as he pointed toward Lee.

"You got nobody else with you?" Silas asked.

"No, just the two of us," Fong answered.

"You're gonna have your work cut out for you," Silas stated. "Don't look like the girl can be much help," he said, pointing toward Lee's bound feet. "It's a hard life mining for gold, even with the missus and three children to help."

"We'll manage," Fong stated. "Is that the boat?"

"Yep, sure is."

The group gathered together, watching as the boat slowly propelled its way toward them. Moments later, the captain shut down the huge steam engine, and silence hung in the air as the boat inched its way toward the dock.

"Pay up and then get your goods loaded," one of the crew members shouted as he jumped off and secured the boat. "If you want help loading, it'll cost you. From the looks of that load, you'd better have somebody lend you a hand," he said to Fong. "With that many supplies, we'll be leaving before you can get it loaded. The fare's ten dollars a person, no food included, and that freight costs eight dollars a ton." "No need to pay for their help," Silas told Fong. "We'll be glad to lend a hand. We can have your goods loaded in no time. Come on, boys," Silas called out to his sons, who were busy skipping rocks on the water.

"Aw, Pa, we was having fun," Ben said, wiping his wet hands on the back of his trousers.

"That's good. And now it's time to work. Ben, you and Lizzy get our supplies loaded. When you get done, come help with the rest of this," he ordered while pointing toward Fong's supplies. "How you planning on getting all these goods to your minin' camp?" Silas asked as he hefted a bag of rice on his shoulder and lifted a crate under his arm.

"I plan to buy a wagon and mules," Fong replied.

"You're gonna pay a pretty price. Should have bought those here in San Francisco. You'd pay a lot less."

"I told you we should have stayed in Chinatown. You don't know anything about gold mining," Lee whispered to her brother. *Can't he see how silly it is to come to a new country and try to do something he knows absolutely nothing about?* she wondered.

"Hi. I'm Lizzy. How old are you?" a small voice asked.

"Twelve," Lee replied, turning toward the girl. Lizzy was dressed in a calico dress, and she wore shoes that looked more like men's work boots than ladies' slippers. Her hair was parted in the middle and woven into two plump, woolly braids, each tied with a strip of blue cloth.

"Me too!" Lizzy replied enthusiastically. Grasping a basket of supplies in each hand, she walked toward the dock. "We can visit once we get on the river," she called back over her shoulder.

Lee smiled and nodded her head. "You sent me another friend," she murmured.

"Who you talkin' to?" the boy called John asked her.

"John! Get those sacks and get moving," Mr. Smith called out to his son, saving Lee from having to give an explanation.

An hour later, the boat edged away from the dock, and the engine began turning the huge paddle wheel, propelling them up the river. As the water churned behind the boat, they gained speed. Soon the countryside turned from dirt and sand to grass-covered rolling hills blanketed in wildflowers of gold, purple, and red. Cool breezes drifted off the river, and the trees along the shore seemed to wave their branches toward the passing boat as it cut through the water, moving farther and farther north. Fong and Silas were busy talking, and it appeared that Mr. Smith was drawing something on a piece of paper. Ben and John were at the rear of the boat watching the paddle wheel plow deeply into the water, its continual circular motion pushing them farther up the river. Mrs. Smith was hard at work mending a dress when Lizzy finally appeared at Lee's side.

"I had to help my mama finish some chores," she said, dropping down beside Lee. "You going to Striker's Gulch?"

"I don't know where we're going. My brother thinks he's going to find gold," Lee replied.

"He might. My papa found some gold. That's how come we were in San Francisco," Lizzy excitedly told her new friend. "Papa says not to tell no one, but I don't figure he'll mind if I tell you."

"How come you can't tell?"

"Don't want no one jumpin' our claim," Lizzy answered. "Don't you know nothin' about gold mining? If folks find out you struck gold, they'll come and try to jump your claim," she continued.

"Oh," was all Lee could think to say. She didn't understand what jumping had to do with gold mining, but she didn't want to admit it. "Did you know there's a small city of Chinese people in San Francisco?" Lee asked, wanting to talk about something other than gold mining.

"No. We never seen no Chinese city, just San Francisco. It's plenty big enough," Lizzy answered. "Where you from, anyway?"

"I'm Chinese," Lee answered.

Lizzy giggled. "I already figured you was Chinese. Just wondered if you been living back East and heard about the gold rush. There's a camp of Chinese miners down river about twenty miles from our place. They came from New York," Lizzy told her.

"No, we're from Canton, China. At least that's where I was

living when we set sail for Gam Saan."

"What's Gam Saan?" Lizzy asked.

"It means 'gold mountain.' That's what my people call California. My people think the streets are paved with gold in your country," Lee explained.

"Ain't never seen gold streets," Lizzy said, shaking her head back and forth.

"I tried to tell my brother, but he wouldn't listen," Lee confided.

"Brothers never listen to their sisters—even when we're right," Lizzy agreed. "Where's your ma and pa?"

"They were killed during a rebellion in our province."

"What's a rebellion?" Lizzy asked before Lee could explain further.

"A battle where people fight and kill each other," Lee answered. "We lived on a small farm north of Canton. There are a lot of battles in the provinces, mostly over land boundaries or different beliefs. My parents were in the fields with my brothers and sisters. They were tending their crops when a band of men from another province came through the countryside killing anyone that was in their path. Fong was living in Canton, and I was back at the house preparing dinner, so we were spared," Lee explained somberly as she recounted the dreadful scene.

"Umm hmm! Didn't they come to the house to see if anyone was left inside?" Lizzy inquired, clinging to every word.

"Yes, but I was a coward and hid," Lee answered, her voice filled with remorse.

"Why you calling yourself a coward and acting like it was wrong to save yourself? If I had been there, I would have hidden," Lizzy stated, shaking her head up and down for emphasis.

Lee shrugged her shoulders. "It just doesn't seem right that they should all be dead while I'm still alive."

"Weren't your time to die. That's what my mama says

when one person dies and another don't. She says there's a time to be born and a time to die. I don't reckon it was your time."

"I suppose not, but it changed everything—and I miss the rest of my family."

Lizzy nodded her head in agreement. "Ain't easy losing people you love, but you got to look on the bright side. You got a chance for a whole new life!"

"I already had a whole new life in Canton. I was living with Mr. and Mrs. Conroy in the European sector of Canton. They're missionaries, and Mrs. Conroy was very nice. She taught me your language, and she taught me about Jesus. I was happy there. But then Fong got this idea about finding gold, which changed everything—again. Mrs. Conroy said I could stay in Canton and live with them until Fong returned to China, but he wouldn't hear of it."

"How come?" Lizzy asked.

"He says we should be together since we are family. But I think it's because he's never going to return to China," Lee confided.

Lizzy glanced toward the back of the boat where her father and Fong continued talking. "Maybe Papa will convince Fong that it's too hard for just the two of you to find gold, and he'll decide to go back home. We could pray about it!"

"I've been praying ever since I found out he wanted to come here, but God doesn't seem to hear me."

"God hears everything. He just ain't answering the way you want. At least not yet," Lizzy replied confidently.

"You think that God might somehow show Fong it's best for us to go home?" Lee asked, her eyes sparkling with enthusiasm.

"He just might. You can't never be sure what God's got in mind," Lizzy replied.

Chapter Six

STRIKER'S GULCH

"I'll be back with a wagon in no time," Silas told Fong when they had unloaded all their belongings off the paddle boat. "You want Lee to come with us?"

"No, she can stay here with me—too hard for her to walk," Fong stated, pointing toward Lee's feet.

Silas nodded and then gathered his family together, walking off toward town. Lee wiggled into a comfortable position on top of the grain sacks, rested her chin in one palm, and stared at her brother.

"Why do you keep looking at me?" Fong finally asked, his irritation obvious.

"I'm wondering when you're going to tell me why we got off the boat. I thought you were going farther north to the American River," she replied.

"After talking to Silas, I decided it was best to stop here."

"But why?" she insisted.

"Silas explained a little more about gold mining—things I didn't know. He convinced me that it would be easier if I spent some time with him. Learning the ropes, he called it. I thought you would be pleased. You'll get to live near Lizzy."

"Yes, but for how long? Until you decide to go searching for gold somewhere else? It's too hard making friends and then losing them. Are we going to stay here for good?"

"I don't know. If we don't find gold, we'll need to move on. We have to have money to live. I'm not going to make any promises I can't keep," he stubbornly insisted.

Lee squinted her eyes against the sun and looked toward the overhanging tree branches that formed an arbor above the road. "It is pretty here," she conceded, observing their peaceful surroundings.

"Does that mean you'll quit your complaining and try to be happy?" Fong asked.

"That depends. I haven't seen our house yet," she replied, not wanting to give in just yet.

Fong grew silent, his eyes fixed on the road as he watched for Mr. Smith. He was deep in thought, so Lee once again settled herself on the mound of supplies and allowed the warm sun to lull her into an afternoon nap.

She was dreaming of their home in China, her parents, and the soldiers with their weapons coming through the fields. But it wasn't her father's shouts that awakened her; it was Mr. Smith calling a team of large gray horses to a halt beside the pile of supplies. The horses snorted and shook their heads as Mr. Smith tied the reins around the wagon's brake handle. Benjamin and John jumped down from the wagon bed and immediately began loading the supplies.

"Sorry for the delay," Silas said as he bounded down. "Had to wait on Mr. Murphy at the livery stable. Otherwise, we'd have been back an hour ago. Did you think we weren't coming back for you?"

"I was beginning to worry a little," Fong admitted as he began heaving supplies into the wagon.

"I wasn't worried. I fell asleep," Lee admitted. "Where's Lizzy?"

"She stayed back in town with her mama. We'll pick them up at the parsonage," Silas explained.

Lee thought about it for a moment and then tugged at Silas's shirtsleeve. "What's a parsonage? I never heard that word before."

Silas gave her a hearty laugh. "It's a house that the church members provide for the preacher. You know about church and preachers?"

"Oh, yes. I lived with missionaries in Canton and learned

about Jesus," she proudly announced. "Fong doesn't believe in Jesus, though."

Silas glanced at Fong and then back at Lee. "Well, I'm glad to know you've heard the Word of God. Maybe your brother will let you attend church services with us on Sundays."

"That would be wonderful, wouldn't it, Fong?" Lee enthusiastically responded.

"We'll see," he mumbled. "Right now my concern is finding a place for us to live."

Silas nodded his head. "You're right, and we're going to do just that. Looks like we have everything. Boys, hop up in the wagon," Silas ordered as he lifted Lee into the back and then hoisted himself onto the seat beside Fong. The boys did as they were told, and the horses once again began clopping down the road. It took less than an hour to reach the outskirts of Striker's Gulch, where Lizzy stood waving at them in front of a white frame house.

"There's Lizzy," Lee shouted, pointing toward her new friend.

"Who cares?" retorted Ben. "All she does is boss me around."

"Watch yourself, young man," Silas sternly ordered as he turned in the seat toward Ben.

"Yes, suh," Ben answered meekly as the wagon came to a halt.

Lee watched from the wagon as a man and woman followed Mrs. Smith from the house and approached the wagon.

"This is our preacher and his wife, Pastor and Mrs. Mitchell," Mrs. Smith announced, looking first at Fong and then back toward Lee.

"Hello. My name is Yung Lee, and this is my brother, Yung Fong. Mr. Smith said maybe I could come to church with them on Sundays," Lee reported. Fong nodded his head, but said nothing.

"We'd like that—and your brother is welcome too," the

preacher replied while giving them a warm smile.

"We should be moving along. It's getting late, and we need to get this wagon unloaded," Silas explained as he helped Mrs. Smith onto the wagon seat. "Get on in there, Lizzy," Silas urged, lifting her high in the air and setting her in the wagon beside Lee.

"Hope to see you Sunday," Pastor Mitchell called after them.

"What's the name of your church?" Lee asked as the horses pulled the wagon into motion.

"It's the First Baptist Church of Striker's Gulch. That's it over there," Lizzy proudly announced, pointing toward a small frame building. "That's the general store—Mr. Potter owns it. And over there's Mrs. Wilson's boardinghouse and laundry. That's the restaurant, and there's the Gold Bar saloon," she continued as they passed the local business establishments.

"And that's Murphy's Livery Stable over there," Silas said to Fong. "I told him we'd bring the wagon and horses back first thing tomorrow."

"Thank you," Fong said. "I can bring them back. I don't want to keep you away from your mining."

"Plenty of time to worry about that come morning," Silas said. "There's going to be lots of work for everybody if we're going to get you settled. You talk to the preacher, Mary?" Silas asked.

"Yes, it's all arranged," she replied.

Lee could hardly contain her excitement when Lizzy announced that they were home. Peeking over the side of the wagon, Lee examined their surroundings. There must be a mistake. Surely the small, rugged cabin wasn't where the Smiths lived. This was California—the gold mountain. Hadn't the Smiths said they had been in San Francisco shopping with the gold they had discovered? That must be it! Now that the Smiths were wealthy, she was sure they would be building a fine home. They just hadn't had time yet.

Mrs. Smith, Lizzy, and Lee went inside while the men busied

themselves unloading the wagon.

"Have a seat," Mrs. Smith offered, pointing toward a wooden bench made from a split log. Each end of the log was nailed to a tree stump, making it just the right height to reach the table. Mrs. Smith quickly started a fire, and the smell of boiling coffee soon filled the room.

"You fixing supper, Mama?" Ben asked as he carried a basket into the room.

"Don't I fix supper every night?"

"Yes. But what you fixin'?" he asked, grinning.

"Thought I might treat you to some ham, fried potatoes, and greens. How does that sound?"

"Mmm hmm. Sounds real good to me," he said, skipping out the door.

When the supplies were finally unloaded from the wagon and stored in a small shed behind the house, Silas, Fong, and the two boys joined the women in the house. Mrs. Smith was busy scooping food into large bowls, which were handed to Lizzy and then placed on the table. A fork and knife had been placed on each of the metal plates that now circled the table.

Unlike her brother, Lee had frequently eaten American food while living with the Conroys. Knowing that this would be a new experience for Fong, she peered down the table toward where he was sitting. He was busy watching what the others did and attempting to mimic their actions. She tried to gain his attention to tell him he wasn't holding his fork and knife properly, but he wouldn't look in her direction. Just as he glanced her way, the piece of ham went sliding across his plate, skittered along the table's edge, and finally landed on the floor beside him. Ben's giggle was brought to an abrupt halt by a stern look from Mr. Smith.

"Don't worry about that," Mrs. Smith said, getting up from where she was seated at one end of the table and quickly retrieving the slice of ham. "Happens to folks all the time." When she returned with Fong's plate, the meat had been cut into bite-sized pieces.

Lee's concern about where they would spend the night was soon settled. Fong and the boys would sleep in the small loft while Lizzy and Lee slept on pallets in front of the stone fireplace. Situated behind a thin curtain at the opposite end of the room was Mr. and Mrs. Smith's bed.

Lee tossed and turned, listening to the night sounds that drifted into the room. A coyote howled in the distance, and Lee huddled closer to Lizzy's sleeping form. The sound of rustling branches scraping across the roof sent chills down her spine. Her eyes grew wide and her body stiffened. Something was under the covers! It was running up and down her leg—a feathery, tickling sensation—probably a giant bug. Carefully, she slid her hand under the blanket and then slapped as hard as she could.

"Yeow! What're you doing?" Lizzy awakened with a holler. "You just about broke my toe."

"I'm sorry. I'm sorry. A spider was crawling on my leg. Look!" Lee whispered, holding up the squished remnants of a velvety black spider between her thumb and forefinger.

"You girls get to sleep," Mrs. Smith called from behind the thin curtain.

"It's okay—just go back to sleep," Lizzy whispered, giving Lee a halfhearted smile.

Burrowing her body into the cornhusk-filled mattress that had been placed on the floor, Lee squeezed her eyes shut and tried to sleep. But no matter how hard she tried, she just couldn't get to sleep—at least not until the sun was beginning to rise in the predawn eastern sky.

"Come on now, time to get up. Lee, get those blankets folded; John, put that mattress on top of the one on our bed; Ben, go fetch me some water; and Lizzy, you get the table set for breakfast," Mrs. Smith ordered while mixing up a batch of biscuits.

After they had finished the morning meal, Lee wandered

outside and sat on a rock above the river while watching Mr. Smith instruct her brother. Mr. Smith was squatting beside a wooden box that he had placed in the river's shallow water. He motioned to Fong, who then pushed his shovel into the river and scooped out a mound of gravel, sand, and dirt that he dumped into the box. Mr. Smith gestured Fong closer, and Lee could see them talking. Fong began pouring a stream of water over the dirt and sand while Mr. Smith pushed and pulled a handle attached at the back of the box.

The rocker box gently swayed back and forth until the gravel was washed clean. The two men held their heads close together and were lifting something out of the box. Probably gold, Lee thought as she leaned forward, attempting to gain a better view. Probably not, she decided when they dumped the contents of the box back into the river.

After several hours, Lee tired of watching the process and made her way back toward the house, where Lizzy and her mother were busy boiling clothes in a large cauldron over an outdoor fire. "I should be helping," Lee said as she approached them.

"You don't need to be helping with this chore," Mrs. Smith replied, pointing down at the bottom of her long dress. It was full of holes, and the hem was ragged. "I don't let Lizzy get around the fire, either. She totes the clothes out back and hangs them on the line to dry."

"Did the fire do all that?" Lee asked, staring at Mrs. Smith's ragged dress.

"Sure did. This here's become my washday dress—can't afford to ruin more than one dress," the older woman replied as she stomped a hot ember that had danced out of the fire and landed nearby. "These are ready to be hung up, Lizzy," Mrs. Smith said as she pulled a shirt from the rinse water with a long wooden paddle and squeezed the excess water back into the kettle.

"Can I help?" Lee asked.

"You can come along and keep me company," Lizzy said, giving her a bright smile. "Mama said to let you enjoy yourself in the fresh air. She said being cooped up on that ship for months on end had to be terrible," she told Lee as the pair moved toward the back of the cabin.

Lee seated herself on a nearby stump and began pulling the clothes from the basket and handing them to Lizzy. "This is sure a peaceful kind of life," Lee remarked while a light breeze blew through the trees and colorful birds warbled their songs back and forth to each other.

"Enjoy it while you can. Come Monday, it's back to school," Lizzy replied.

"School's not over for the year?" Lee asked, somewhat disheartened. "How come you were in San Francisco if school's still going on?"

"We got almost three months of school left, and Papa said we couldn't wait. He wanted to get his gold assayed, and Mama needed supplies she couldn't buy in Striker's Gulch. We'll have to make up the lessons we missed," Lizzy explained.

"What's assayed? Is that something special you get done to your gold?"

Lizzy shook her head. "You sure don't know nothing about gold mining, do you? It means 'tested.' They got special people who can check to make sure your gold is genuine and tell you what it's worth."

"I guess I don't know anything about gold mining, but I'll learn. I'm a real good student," Lee replied.

"That's good, but I'd put my head to learning at school and forget about the gold mining—at least for now."

School! That meant more new people and new places. She didn't want to go to school in Striker's Gulch.

Chapter Seven

Lee longed for a time when she could talk privately to her brother. She wasn't sure what plans he was making for their future, but it didn't appear they were going to move far from the Smiths. Just last night, she had overheard Fong and Mr. Smith talk about building a small cabin as soon as school was closed down for the summer. With John and Ben to help, Mr. Smith figured they could have a cabin constructed in short order. But there were three more months until the end of the school term. Surely Fong would have enough gold for them to return to China by then, and surely Mr. and Mrs. Smith would move to a grand new home in the city.

"Have a good day," Mrs. Smith called out as Ben slapped the reins, finally convincing their old mule to move. The small wooden cart rocked back and forth as they maneuvered down the road toward Striker's Gulch.

"Is this how you get to school every day—in the wagon, I mean?" Lee asked her companions.

Ben shook his head and looked at her as though she didn't have sense enough to come in out of the rain. "'Course. How else did you think we'd get to school? It's too far to walk and we ain't got no riding horses."

"You don't have to talk so mean, Ben Smith. If you was in China, you wouldn't have any idea how to get to school," Lizzy chided.

Lee smiled at her friend. "It's all right, Lizzy. I thought Fong and Mr. Smith would need the wagon while they're mining for gold."

"Naw, don't need no wagon when you're mining down at

the river—just a sluice, running water, and a strong back. Besides, they couldn't get this wagon down the hillside to the river, even if they wanted to," John explained as they continued to bump down the dusty road.

"I think I got a splinter," Ben whined after sliding across the wagon's rough lumber seat.

"Serves you right after the way you talked to Lee. You better pull it out," Lizzy ordered indifferently. "If you don't, it'll just fester up and get sore. You better hurry up—we're almost there. The bell is already ringing."

"I'm scared," Lee whispered in Lizzy's ear.

"It's okay. Most everybody's nice. 'Course there's a few of the boys that are mean, and some of the town girls don't think we're as good as them," she said.

Just then, John came around the side of the wagon and lifted Lee down. "Want me to carry you?" he asked. "I don't mind," he added quickly.

"Maybe if you'd walk beside me in case I lose my balance," she replied.

John, Lizzy, and Ben formed a semicircle around Lee, and they slowly walked the short distance to the school. A few of the children stood watching as they approached the entrance. Suddenly, Lee stopped in her tracks. There were steps—three of them—and no railing to hold onto. She looked up at John. "Here we go," he said, hoisting her into his arms and then quickly depositing her inside the door.

The four of them walked into the schoolhouse. Lizzy slid behind one of the desks near the front of the room. "You can sit beside me," she instructed, patting the wooden seat.

Lee slipped onto the seat beside her, hoping to be ignored. But she feared that wasn't going to happen. As the children began gathering in the classroom, she could hear them whispering about her feet. She hunkered down in the seat, wishing that she could become invisible.

"It works best if you just ignore them," Lizzy whispered in

Lee's ear while giving her an encouraging smile.

"Why?" Lee asked.

"If you show them it bothers you, they'll just keep it up longer," Lizzy explained.

One of the bigger boys came and stood beside their desk. "Be seated," the teacher instructed as she walked toward the front of the room.

The boy dropped down beside Lee, giving her a giant shove toward Lizzy as he seated himself. Lee was squashed between her friend and the unknown boy, while Lizzy clung to the edge of the desk in order to keep from falling on the floor.

"Quit it!" Lee whispered when the boy pushed even harder.

He gave her an evil grin, revealing a wide gap between his two front teeth. His bright red hair pointed in every direction, and his face was covered with little reddish-brown spots.

"Don't make no trouble, or you'll be sorry," he warned. "You sure are ugly. I bet you don't even know how ugly you are," he scowled, jamming his needlelike elbow into Lee's side.

"I was wondering—did you spend the night spinning on your head to do that?" Lee countered while pointing at the boy's unkempt hair.

"Howard! What are you doing sitting there? Get back in your seat," the teacher ordered. Lee breathed a sigh of relief as the boy rose from the desk and slowly shuffled toward the back of the classroom. "It appears that we have a new student in class today. Stand up and tell us your name."

Lee stood up and held onto the desk. "I am Yung Lee from Canton, China. My brother and I now live in Striker's Gulch," she answered in her very best English.

The teacher glanced at Lee's feet. "You may be seated, Yung. We are glad to have you in class, and I am pleased that you speak English. Children, please welcome Yung to our class."

"Welcome, Yung," the children all repeated in unison.

Lizzy quickly raised her hand. "Miss Thompson, her name is Yung Lee, but she is called Lee."

Miss Thompson looked from Lizzy toward Lee, who was nodding her head up and down. "In China, the family name comes first," she explained. "I am Yung Lee and my brother is Yung Fong, but I am called Lee and he is called Fong."

"And Yung ain't gonna live long enough to grow old, if she don't watch out," a male voice from the back of the room threatened.

"That will do!" Miss Thompson warned. "Thank you, Lee, for sharing that interesting information with the class. Now, let's get started with our studies. As you all know, we've spent a good deal of time this year working on our writing skills. I think the time has arrived to see how much you have learned. I want each of you to write an essay, which you will be required to read in class. For you younger children, a one-page report will be fine, but I expect at least three well-written pages from the rest of the class. Any questions?"

"What are we supposed to write about?" one of the younger children asked.

"It's your choice, but the essays must be completed two weeks from today. Each day I will choose four students to read in front of the class," Miss Thompson explained. "Any other questions?"

"What happens if we don't do it?" the red-haired boy called out from the back of the room.

"Then I'll have to visit with your father, Howard," Miss Thompson calmly replied. "Class, please open your reading books to page thirty-eight. Margaret, stand and begin reading at the top of the page," she ordered.

Lee was thankful that the teacher hadn't called on her to read in front of the class. Not that she couldn't read as well as the other students she had listened to throughout the day—in fact, she could have performed more capably than many of them. But she knew from the treatment she had received during recess and lunchtime that she was going to be singled out as the scapegoat—at least for a while.

"You shouldn't have talked back to Howard O'Laughlin," Lizzy remarked on the way home that evening. "He's mean—really mean. Nobody disagrees with Howard."

"You're right, Lizzy. I should have just ignored him or said something kind. That's probably what Jesus would have done. Sometimes it's so hard for me to do the right thing. It's as though the words slip out of my mouth on their own," Lee admitted. "Mrs. Conroy told me that the best way to stop someone like Howard was to treat him with kindness. I'll have to try harder."

Can I be kind to Howard O'Laughlin the rest of the school year? Lee wondered. She knew it wouldn't be easy. Why hadn't Fong allowed her to remain with the Conroys? Then she wouldn't have to put up with mean-spirited people like Howard O'Laughlin.

* * *

Two weeks had passed. Each morning Lee prayed that she could make it through one more day without saying something mean to Howard. Meanwhile, he continually taunted her, making fun of her tiny feet, the color of her skin, her accent, her slanted eyes, her clothes, or anything else that he thought would make her angry.

Lee disregarded Lizzy's suggestion to remain silent when Howard made his nasty remarks. Instead, she smiled sweetly and said, "Jesus loves you, Howard O'Laughlin." At first it made him angry and he taunted her even more. But the last few days, he had ignored her, so she thought her prayer had been answered.

"Lee, I'd like you to read your essay to the class," Miss Thompson announced. Lee's head snapped to attention. Suddenly it felt as though a basketful of butterflies were bouncing around in her stomach. It was her turn and she was prepared, so why did she feel so frightened?

Lizzy turned and gave her a reassuring smile. Lee tried to return the smile, but her lips wouldn't seem to move. Slowly, she walked to the front of the classroom and then turned toward the sea of faces staring back at her. Howard O'Laughlin leaned forward across his desk, giving her a look of gleeful anticipation.

Taking a deep breath, she began. "My composition is entitled 'Bound Feet.' In China it is a custom to bind the feet of very young girls. Tiny feet are considered a thing of beauty in my homeland." Lee heard Howard snicker, but she ignored him and continued to read. Her voice sounded strange and quivery. *Help me get through this*, she prayed silently. With each paragraph her voice grew stronger; soon the butterflies were no longer fluttering around in her stomach.

"The front part of the foot is folded down and back toward the heel. Then it is tightly bound with strips of fabric. This causes the arch to break." She heard several gasps, but she didn't look up. "Throughout the centuries, women have endured pain in order to be considered beautiful by the standards and customs of their countries. Women in Europe and the United States sometimes wear very tight corsets to have small waists. Often, the tight corsets cause them to faint or break their ribs. In African countries women pierce and adorn their lips and ears, stretching them out of shape. In China, we bind feet.

"All of these customs alter the way people look on the outside, but I believe it is not so important how we look on the outside. Inner beauty is much more important, and we can all change what's in here," she continued, pointing to her heart for emphasis. "What is more important—the size of my feet, or the fact that I treat you kindly? The color of my skin, or the fact that I tell the truth? The shape of my eyes, or the fact that I treat you with respect? My difficulty pronouncing English words, or the fact that my words are spoken in love? That my traditions are different from yours, or the fact that I honor your right to have different customs?"

She paused for a moment. The class was very quiet. Bravely she raised her eyes and was met by one of Lizzy's toothy grins. Lee returned the smile and once again began to read.

"In China, many families have a teacup that is passed from generation to generation. It is highly valued because it is a symbol of our tradition and heritage. This is the one that belongs to my family," she proudly announced, pulling the cloth-wrapped teacup from her lunch pail. Peeling back the covering, she lifted the china teacup high into the air.

"You can see that the china is very thin and the mouth of the cup is larger than a regular coffee cup," she explained. "This is the teacup that has been used in my family to measure the size of our women's bound feet for many generations. The foot must be small enough to place across the top of the cup without touching the rim."

"Let's see you do it," one of the boys called from the back of the room.

"Would you like to help?" Lee asked him.

"Is it okay?" the boy inquired, looking toward Miss Thompson.

"Certainly. Why don't you sit here," the teacher instructed, moving a wooden bench to where Lee stood. "If you'd like to take turns gathering around, it will be easier to see," she told the class.

After seating herself, Lee handed her teacup to the boy. Carefully, he placed the bottom of her foot across the rim of the teacup. The children rose from their desks and were straining to gain a better view.

"It really does fit!" one of the younger girls declared in an awestruck voice.

The room filled with sounds of amazement and wonder as the students continued to observe the sight. "So she's a freak. We all knew that anyway," Howard O'Laughlin boomed from the rear of the class. A deafening silence followed.

"Howard!" Miss Thompson's voice filled the room. "See me after school," she ordered.

"Ain't ya gonna sit me in the corner?" he heckled.

"No, Howard. Just see me after school," Miss Thompson repeated, her bright blue eyes momentarily flashing with anger. "Any other questions for Lee?" the teacher inquired, turning back toward the rest of the class.

"Does it hurt?" Nora Ellerby asked.

"Yes," Lee answered honestly.

"But it quits hurtin' after a while, doesn't it?" Nora continued.

"No. Bound feet always hurt, but after a while, you don't notice it so much—unless you have to walk a lot," she added.

"All right, class, let's be seated. Thank you, Lee, for a very informative composition. Your reading and writing skills are excellent," Miss Thompson praised.

Lee wrapped the teacup, placed it in her lunch pail, and carried it back to her desk. Lizzy was beaming as Lee approached their desk. "You did real good. Miss Thompson's gonna give you a good grade. I could tell she liked your essay," she whispered.

"Thank you," Lee whispered in return. *And thank You, Jesus*, she silently prayed.

"Take out your slates or spelling boards. Today we're going to work on several new words," Miss Thompson instructed.

The rest of the morning passed in a blur. It seemed as though Lee had just completed reading her essay when Miss Thompson announced that they were dismissed for lunch. There was a flurry of commotion as most of the class grabbed their lunch pails and ran outdoors. However, Lizzy and Lee chose to remain at their desks while eating thick slices of homemade bread slathered with Mrs. Smith's wild plum preserves.

"Your essay has been the best so far," Lizzy said, replacing the lid on her pail. "Want to go outdoors and sit on the steps? It's real nice outside."

"Mmm hmm," Lee replied, licking a blob of jam from her lips. "Let's go."

Several of the boys were taking turns climbing a nearby tree while some of the other children were playing a rousing game of toss over. Lee watched as a group of children stood lined up along each side of the schoolhouse. One of the children would throw a ball, hoping it would go over the roof. The children waiting on the other side had to catch the ball and successfully return it. "You can go and play if you want to," Lee offered.

"I'd rather stay here and talk to you," Lizzy replied, scooting a little closer as Howard walked toward them. He gave Lizzy a little shove as he reached the top of the steps and entered the classroom. "Wonder why he's so anxious to get back inside."

"Maybe he's going to talk to Miss Thompson about his behavior while I was reading my essay," Lee ventured.

"I don't think so. I saw Miss Thompson and Mary Louise go to fetch water. They haven't returned yet."

"Do you think what I wrote in my composition will change the way Howard and the others treat us?" Lee asked.

"I hope so, but I'm not counting on it," Lizzy replied. "Pa says it's hard for people to accept folks who are different. And you and me, we're different."

"That's true enough. But so are Ben and John, and the other boys choose them to play on their teams," Lee replied, pointing toward Lizzy's brothers playing alongside the others.

"It's not so much because they like my brothers. It's because John is good at playing games. His team always wins. They know that if they don't let Ben play, John won't play, either," Lizzy confided.

"Oh," Lee replied. It was the only thing she could think to say.

"You're disappointed to hear that, aren't you? You thought

maybe the color of my brothers' skin didn't matter to the other boys, didn't you?" Lizzy asked.

Lee nodded her head.

"Well, the truth of the matter is that if John played like Ben McVicar, they would never pick him to be on a team. It ain't right, but that's the way it is."

"You two sure make an ugly sight," Howard sneered as he walked past them and went back down the steps.

"Jesus loves you, Howard," Lee called after him.

Howard turned and gave a nasty laugh. "You think so?" he asked before striding off toward a group of boys across the schoolyard. The girls watched the group huddle together. Several of the boys looked in their direction as Howard stood talking to them.

"I wonder what he's telling those boys. The way they keep looking over here, I think it must be about us," Lizzy decided.

"Why would they be talking about us? We've done nothing to them," Lee stated.

"Maybe 'cause Howard has to stay after school to talk to Miss Thompson," Lizzy suggested.

"But that's his own fault for being rude during class. It has nothing to do with us."

"That's what you think. You're the one who was reading when he got in trouble. To Howard's way of thinking, that makes it your fault," Lizzy explained.

"I hope not," Lee answered. Surely Lizzy was confused. How could it be her fault that Howard behaved badly?

Two more students read their essays during the afternoon session—Ruth Morrison and Howard O'Laughlin. Ruth's theme was a three-page instruction on the art of quilting; Howard's was a poorly written paragraph on catching frogs.

"Is that all?" Miss Thompson asked when Howard began to shuffle back toward his desk.

"Yup. Couldn't make it no longer 'cause that's all there is to finding frogs and catching 'em," he replied with a smirk.

"Then you should have chosen another topic," Miss Thompson admonished. "That wasn't an acceptable composition, Howard. I expect you to prepare a new one."

"I don't know how to do it any better," he retorted.

"Just follow Lee's example from this morning," the teacher instructed. "Select a topic that may be expanded upon and that teaches a lesson. That shouldn't be too difficult."

"I just taught you how to catch frogs. That's an important lesson," he argued as his friends burst into laughter.

"That will do!" Miss Thompson ordered while she drummed her fingers on top of the wood desk.

"Howard, I do not intend to debate this topic with you. I expect another essay. We'll discuss it after school. Now, sit down!"

That afternoon, Howard sneered at Lee and Lizzy as they were leaving school for the day. "See ya tomorrow," he taunted in a menacing voice.

"You don't frighten me, Howard," Lee replied.

"You just wait. You're gonna pay for getting me in trouble."

"I didn't get you in trouble. You got yourself in trouble," Lee shot back.

"Come on, Lee. Don't bother talking to him. It won't do any good," Lizzy urged.

"She's right. There ain't nothin' you can say that's gonna do you any good," Howard scowled.

Lee tried to chase Howard's threats from her mind as they rode home. After all, what could he do to her? Miss Thompson or some of the other children were always close at hand, and Howard didn't live nearby.

"Looks like you're gonna get to help Ma finish making the soap," John called over his shoulder as they approached the cabin. Mrs. Smith was standing beside a large kettle hanging on a tripod over a fire outside the house.

"I'm glad I ain't a girl," Ben laughed as he jumped down from the wagon.

"John, your pa wants you and Ben down below. He and Fong are building a new sluice, and he needs your help. Hurry up," their mother prodded.

"Aw, Ma, I'm hungry. Can't we eat something first?" Ben begged.

"No time for eating. Get on down there," she ordered.

"I'm glad I ain't a boy," Lizzy teased as he shuffled past her on his way down the hill.

"Lizzy, don't dawdle over there by the wagon. Get inside and change your clothes. I need you to help me finish pouring this soap into the molds."

"Can I help?" Lee asked while hobbling toward Mrs. Smith.

"It's better if you're not too close to the fire, Lee. You might lose your balance and get burned," Mrs. Smith warned. "Why don't you go inside and set the table for supper? That would be a big help."

"Yes, ma'am," Lee forlornly replied. She'd rather stay outdoors with Lizzy and Mrs. Smith, but she didn't argue.

It didn't take long to place the metal utensils, plates, and cups on the table. A vase with pretty flowers would have brightened the room, but Mrs. Smith didn't seem to mind if things were plain. Besides, it would be impossible for Lee to go wandering through the woods looking for wildflowers. The sound of laughter pulled her from her thoughts of wildflower decorations and lured her to the door of the cabin. Mesmerized, she stood watching Lizzy and Mrs. Smith in animated conversation. Stabs of envy raced through her when she noticed Mrs. Smith lean down and place a soft kiss on Lizzy's cheek.

It seemed like forever since she had felt the warmth of her mother's hug or a tender kiss, and Fong certainly wasn't going to give her a hug. He never showed any emotion—except anger. Whenever Lee inquired about his luck at finding gold, he became angry; whenever she expressed a desire to return to Canton, he became angry; whenever she talked about their family, he became angry; and, whenever she asked how long they were going to live with the Smiths, he became angry. At first she had been surprised at her brother's willingness to live and work with another family. She thought that he would want a gold claim of his own. But soon she realized the men must have reached an agreement that they could accomplish more working together, rather than apart. Not that she wanted to move away from the Smiths—Lizzy was a wonderful friend. She just wanted to know what plans Fong was making for their future and if he was considering a return to China.

"All finished?" Mrs. Smith called to her.

"Yes, ma'am," she replied, attempting to smile.

"The men went into town today. Got something special for you," Mrs. Smith said. Lee watched as Lizzy's mother dug deeply into the pocket of her apron and pulled something out. "You got some mail today. Take this to Lee," she ordered Lizzy as she handed her daughter the letter. "You can read it while we finish up out here. We're almost done."

Lee looked down at the envelope and immediately recognized the handwriting—Mrs. Conroy's. She hadn't forgotten. After all these months of waiting, Lee had finally received a letter. Carefully opening the envelope, she was greeted by a familiar smell that wafted through the air and tickled her nose. Delighted, she pulled the letter from its envelope and inhaled deeply. Mrs. Conroy's perfume. It's my hug. And just when I needed it. She devoured every word of the letter and then began reading it again.

"Is your letter from Mrs. Conroy?" Lizzy asked, skipping into the cabin. "Does she miss you? Is she coming to California to visit?" she continued, without waiting for answers to her questions.

"It's not polite to stick your nose in other people's business," Mrs. Smith chided.

"It's all right," Lee grinned. "It's from Mrs. Conroy. She says that she and Mr. Conroy both miss me very much. She's glad

I'm attending school. I'm supposed to tell her all about my lessons the next time I write."

"What else does it say?" Lizzy questioned, plopping down in front of Lee.

"She's very happy that I'm living with fine Christian people like the Smiths, and she's especially glad that I have a wonderful new friend named Lizzy," Lee reported.

"She knows about me?" Lizzy beamed.

"Of course! You're my best friend, Lizzy. How could I write a letter without telling about you?"

"Supper ready?" Mr. Smith asked, ducking his head as he walked through the doorway. "You get your letter?" he asked Lee, without waiting for an answer to his first question.

"Yes, sir. It's from Mrs. Conroy."

"Mrs. Conroy's real happy that Lee's living with Christian folks like us, and she's extra happy that I'm her friend," Lizzy proudly told her father.

"Good. That's real good," he said, giving both girls a big smile. "Let's say the blessing and have us some supper. I worked up a big appetite today," he added while patting his stomach.

"You have a big appetite every day," Mrs. Smith replied.

He gave her a hearty laugh and then bowed his head. "Father, I thank You for this food and this family. I thank You for our health and happiness and for the friendship of Fong and Lee. Bless this food to our bodies and use us as You see fit. Amen."

"Lee read her composition in class today. Miss Thompson said it was excellent," Lizzy announced as the bowls of food were passed around the table.

"That's wonderful, Lee," Mrs. Smith praised.

"I took my teacup and showed them how it was used to measure the size of my feet," Lee added.

"That was a good idea. Sometimes it helps to see an example," Mr. Smith chimed in.

"You took the teacup to school?" Fong asked in an angry voice. "What if it had been broken? That was very foolish, Lee."

"You don't even care if I do well in school. All you care about is finding gold. Besides, the cup didn't get broken. It's wrapped in a cloth in my lunch pail," Lee answered.

"In your lunch pail?" Mrs. Smith asked, a startled look crossing her face.

"Yes. Over there," Lee answered, pointing to one of the tin pails lined up on the shelf across the room.

"I've opened all the lunch pails, Lee. Your cup wasn't in there," Mrs. Smith quietly replied.

"What? It has to be. I put it in there myself. You saw me, didn't you, Lizzy?" she asked. Her breathing became shallow as she turned toward Lizzy for confirmation. It felt as though a thousand drums were thundering inside her chest.

Lizzy nodded. "You put it in there. I saw you," she agreed.

Lee looked at her brother. His face was filled with rage. "You are an irresponsible child. I can trust you with nothing!" he shouted before jumping up from the table and rushing outside.

The pleasure of Miss Thompson's remarks and Mrs. Conroy's letter was gone—stamped out by Fong's angry remarks and the fear that her teacup really was missing.

"Are you sure it's not there?" Lee asked Mrs. Smith. "I don't understand how it could disappear."

The two girls sat staring across the table at each other. Then, as if hit by a bolt of lightening, they sat up straight and shouted out in unison, "Howard O'Laughlin!"

"Howard O'Laughlin? What's he got to do with this?" Mr. Smith asked.

"He went into the classroom when everyone was outside at lunchtime. Not even Miss Thompson was in there," Lizzy explained.

"That don't mean he took it," Ben replied.

"That's true. But you didn't hear all the things he was saying to Lee today, either. He's got it. I just know he does," Lizzy told her brother.

"Don't want to be falsely accusing no one," her father admonished. "Best thing to do is ask him if he's seen it," Mr. Smith advised Lee.

"I don't think he'll admit to having it," Lee meekly replied. "He doesn't like me," she added.

"Why not?" Mrs. Smith inquired.

"He says I'm ugly. I don't think he likes foreigners."

Mrs. Smith laughed. "Just about everyone in this country's a foreigner. O'Laughlin sounds like it might be an Irish name. If his family comes from Ireland, that makes him a foreigner too."

"But his skin is white and his eyes are round," Lee replied.

Mr. and Mrs. Smith gave each other a knowing glance. It was obvious that they realized Howard O'Laughlin was a young man filled with prejudice against anything or anybody that was different. Black skin had caused them to endure their share of prejudice too.

"Can't pay no mind to folks who think like that. The good Lord made all of us, so I figure He must like variety," Mr. Smith stated.

Lee smiled at that idea—she liked variety too. But that didn't change the fact that her teacup was missing. And Howard O'Laughlin was most likely the person who had it.

Chapter Eight

"Maybe I should tell Miss Thompson," Lee said as they approached the schoolhouse the next morning.

"I don't think so. If Howard has your cup and he gets in trouble with Miss Thompson, he'll probably never return it. Or worse yet, he'll break it," Lizzy replied. "You know how mean he is."

Lee nodded. "You think I should ask him if he has it?"

"That's what Pa said. I don't think he'll admit it, but it's worth a try. Wait until we go out for recess," Lizzy suggested.

Lee glanced back toward Howard and shuddered at his sinister grin. It was impossible to concentrate on anything that Miss Thompson was saying. When recess finally arrived, she wondered if she would be brave enough to approach Howard. But once they were outside, she knew that she wouldn't need to gather her courage and ask if he had the teacup. Howard was leaning against the trunk of a large sycamore tree, the fragile teacup swinging back and forth on one of his fingers.

"Look, Lizzy," she whispered, nudging her friend in the side. "Howard's got my teacup."

"Oh, no! I hope he doesn't drop it. What you gonna do?"

"I don't know," Lee answered. She was afraid to look away for fear that the teacup would once again disappear. Cautiously she motioned for Howard to come to where they were sitting. To her surprise, he ambled toward them and came to a halt directly in front of her.

"May I please have my teacup?" Lee asked in her sweetest voice. She didn't want to upset him.

80

Howard gave an evil laugh. "Oh, sure. I stole this thing out of your lunch pail, and now I'm going to hand it right back, just because you asked," he jeered. "You're as stupid as you are ugly."

"I'm not stupid and I'm not ugly," Lee bristled. "It's my cup and you should return it."

Several of Howard's friends gathered around them. "Where's Miss Thompson?" one of them asked.

"Don't worry. She went into town for something and left Margaret in charge," Howard gloated. "Little Miss Tiny Feet says I oughtta give her this teacup back," Howard mockingly reported to his friends. "What do you guys think?"

They all laughed in unison. "Hey, Howard, let's see if you can get your foot inside that teacup," one of the boys dared.

"Why didn't I think of that?" he scoffed. "'In my country, tiny feet are a sign of beauty,'" he mimicked, placing the cup on the ground. He lifted his foot into the air, the heavy work boot balanced above the cup.

"Please, don't!" Lee begged, trembling with fear.

"'Please, don't,'" Howard taunted, lifting his leg even higher into the air. Lee watched as his leg hurled downward and stomped the ground. His huge work boot had landed only inches away from her precious teacup. Pointing at Lee, the boys burst into gales of laughter.

"I scared her so bad she almost turned white," Howard remarked, joining in their laughter.

"Hey, here comes Miss Thompson back from town," one of the boys warned. Howard grabbed the cup, and the group of boys circled around him as they walked back toward the tree.

"Is there a problem?" Miss Thompson asked as she approached the two girls sitting on the steps.

Lee could see Howard holding her teacup high in the air. If she told Miss Thompson, he might send the cup smashing to the ground. So she merely shook her head. "No, Miss Thompson, there's no problem." It was a lie. She hoped God would understand that she didn't want Howard to break her teacup.

"It's a good thing you didn't tattle," Howard muttered as he walked past Lee and entered the classroom.

"We're going to be taking some special tests for the rest of the day," Miss Thompson announced to the class. "We only have a few months of school left, but I'm afraid some of you are lagging behind in your studies." Her announcement was met by groans from most of the students. "It won't be that bad. Most of you will breeze through this in no time at all. Once you've finished, you can leave for the day," she promised.

She had been right. Lizzy and Lee were finished and sitting on the steps when Benjamin and John appeared some time later. By mid-afternoon most of the students were pouring out of the classroom, pleased to be on their way.

"Pa's gonna be happy to see us home early," John stated.

"Howard still in school?" Lizzy asked as John lifted her into the back of the wagon.

"Yeah. Howard and a couple of his friends are about all that's left in there. He ain't too smart," Ben replied.

"Smart enough to have my teacup," Lee told them.

"You sure he's got it?" John asked.

"Oh, yes. He's got it, and he made sure I knew it." On the ride home, the girls took turns recounting Howard's antics during recess.

"I can get it from him," John remarked as they were nearing home. "Howard's no match for me, and he knows it."

"No. You'll get in trouble, John. Besides, I think he would break the teacup before he'd agree to hand it over to you. But thank you for wanting to help," Lee added.

"So you're just gonna let him keep it?" John asked.

"No. I'm going to pray about it. Maybe if we all pray about it, Howard will give it back."

"That sounds like a good idea," Lizzy replied. "I'll pray about it, too."

"You don't always get what you pray for," Ben muttered from the front seat.

"That's true enough, but praying can't hurt," John told his brother. "Okay, Lee. We'll all be praying that Howard will have a change of heart and return your cup."

"But I wouldn't hold my breath," Ben chimed in as he jumped down from the wagon.

"What you all doing home so early?" Mrs. Smith called out. "Everybody okay?"

"We're fine, Mama. Miss Thompson gave us a test today, and we were allowed to leave school when we finished," Lizzy explained. "You got some chores for me, or should I start on my homework?"

"You and Lee go ahead with your schoolwork. John and Ben, check with your pa and see if he's needing any help," their mother instructed.

The two boys ambled down the hillside toward the riverbed where their father and Fong were hard at work, shoveling and washing the gravel in search of gold.

"Any luck finding your teacup?" Mrs. Smith asked Lee.

"Howard has it. He won't give it back, so we're going to pray about it. Would you pray too?" Lee requested.

"Yes, I'll pray, but tell me what happened today," she said, sitting down beside Lee. Listening intently, she appeared shocked when Lee told of Howard's behavior earlier that day.

"That boy needs to be taught some manners," she responded angrily. "I think we should talk to Miss Thompson—or maybe his parents."

"Oh, please don't do that," Lee begged. "I don't want him to break my cup. Could we pray about it—at least for a few days?"

"I suppose, if that's what you want," Mrs. Smith answered. "But if you change your mind, I want you to tell me."

"I promise," Lee replied, giving her a relieved smile.

*   *   *

A week later, Howard O'Laughlin appeared in school with a purplish-yellow shiner on his left eye and a split lower lip. That same day, Miss Thompson announced that she was making some seating changes.

The class listened carefully as Miss Thompson began calling out names and moving the students to their new seating assignments. Lee was forlorn when Lizzy was told to move beside Matthew Dowd.

"Howard O'Laughlin, come sit beside Yung Lee," Miss Thompson ordered. Lee's stomach flip-flopped. Of all the people in the class, why did it have to be Howard O'Laughlin? She felt dizzy as she listened to the scraping of his boots approaching her desk. "Sit down, Howard," Miss Thompson commanded firmly. He fell into the seat beside her, his legs sprawling out into the aisle. "These seating assignments are permanent until the end of the school year," Miss Thompson continued.

"Until the end of the year?" Matthew Dowd groaned from the rear of the room.

"Don't that make you happy?" Howard sneered.

"Miss Thompson," Margaret called out as she waved her arm high in the air.

"Yes, Margaret?"

"May I ask why you are doing this?"

"I have graded the test I gave you last week. Some students didn't perform very well while other students had exceptional results. It is my hope that all of you will pass to a higher grade level at the end of the school year. However, I fear this won't occur unless the students who are having difficulty receive additional help. Since the amount of time I can spend with each student is limited, it is my hope that you will help each other."

So Miss Thompson expected her to help Howard O'Laughlin with his schoolwork. Lee could feel him gawking at her. She returned his stare. The strap of his overalls hung down off his shoulder, and his red plaid shirt was ripped and dirty. A tiny slit was all that remained open behind his swollen eyelid, and the angry purple color was streaked with lines of red and orangish-yellow shading.

"I want you to begin working on your spelling words," Miss Thompson instructed a short time later.

"What happened to your eye?" Lee asked, placing her slate on top of the desk.

"What do you think happened to my eye?"

"It looks like someone got the best of you in a fist fight," Lee sweetly replied.

"Ain't nobody gets the best of me in a fist fight," Howard angrily retorted. "I weren't fighting. Miss Thompson came to our house and told my pa I was getting bad grades in school. Soon as she left, my pa whipped me."

"Your pa did that to you?" Lee was stunned. She attempted to hide her astonishment, but she knew it was too late. Howard had seen it in her eyes and heard it in her voice.

"I don't need your pity, so don't you go feeling sorry for me. I'd rather have my pa hitting me the rest of my life than spend one day looking like you," he nastily replied.

Lee stared at him for a long moment. "Well, I don't think you need to worry about looking like me, but you do need to worry about how much help I'm going to give you with your schoolwork."

"What's that supposed to mean? You heard Miss Thompson. She said you have to help me so I can pass to the next grade."

Lee thought she saw a flicker of fear in the eye that wasn't swollen. "I think I can be a big help to you, Howard. I can even help you write a good essay."

"Then get busy and start writing it," he ordered.

"That's not the way it works, Howard. I said I *could* help you. I didn't say I *would* help you," Lee replied.

"What do you mean, stupid?"

"If I were you, I wouldn't be calling anyone else stupid. If you expect any help from me, stop calling me names. Do you understand?" she asked. She was surprised when he slowly nodded his head in agreement. "As soon as you return my teacup, we'll begin working on your lessons," she said calmly.

"Oh, no you don't," he muttered under his breath. "You're not getting that teacup back until my essay is written and I pass my math test."

"You don't understand, Howard. You need me; I don't need you. When I receive my undamaged teacup, we will begin working on your lessons," Lee answered in a hushed voice.

"How are you two doing?" Miss Thompson asked as she neared the desk where they sat side by side.

"Fine, we're doing just fine. Aren't we, Howard?" Lee said, giving Miss Thompson a smile as she continued down the row of desks.

"I'll bring your teacup in the morning," Howard finally conceded. "But you better keep your promise, or you'll have a shiner on both your eyes when I get through with you," he threatened.

"You keep your word, Howard, and I'll keep mine," Lee assured him.

All the way to school the next morning, Lee prayed that Howard would keep his word and return the teacup. She wanted to retrieve this valued family heirloom, but more than that, she wanted to mend her relationship with Fong. Except to make a daily inquiry about the missing teacup, Fong hadn't spoken to her since the incident. Each day when she reported her lack of success, he would merely shake his head in disgust and walk away. Perhaps today she would be able to say the words that he wanted to hear.

Lee sat at her desk, waiting for Howard to appear. As usual, he charged into the room at the very last minute.

"Did you bring it?" Lee asked as he flopped down beside her.

"Quiet!" Miss Thompson commanded from the front of the room as she rapped her desk with a long wooden stick.

Chapter Nine

"We'll begin with our geography lesson this morning," Miss Thompson said as she pointed to a large map that had been tacked to the wall. "I have several games and rhymes that we're going to use to help us remember the capitals of each country," their teacher enthusiastically continued. Lee clapped her hands in delight; she thought it was a wonderful idea. Howard crouched down in his seat; he thought the idea stank.

An hour later, when Miss Thompson announced that they had completed their geography lesson for the day, Lee gave Howard a sidelong glance. She certainly wasn't looking forward to devoting the rest of her day to helping Howard with his studies. But Howard gave her a grin and released a huge sigh of relief when the teacher instructed the student tutors to begin working with their assigned classmates.

"I'm not going to help you until I see my teacup," Lee insisted, folding her arms in front of her. Then she gazed straight ahead and remained silent.

"I'll show it to you at lunchtime. I can't pull it out of my lunch pail right here in the middle of class. Miss Thompson would skin me alive," Howard argued.

Lee continued to stare toward the front of the classroom. "I might like to watch that," she retorted, a tiny smile playing at the corner of her mouth.

"Come on! Let's get started before I get in more trouble," Howard urged.

"I'll help you a little, but only until lunchtime. Start writing your essay, and I'll read it and help you correct it," she ordered.

"You tell me what to write, and I'll put it down on the paper," Howard countered.

"I'm not going to do that. It's supposed to be your essay. Now start writing."

"You're making me work on my stupid story so you don't have to do nothin' for me before lunchtime, ain't ya?" Howard questioned, a spark of understanding in his eyes.

"You're right, Howard. But even though you've figured out my plan, it doesn't change anything," Lee said as she smiled.

"Lee, what are you and Howard working on?" Miss Thompson asked as she approached their desk.

"I've asked him to begin his composition. I told him I would read and then help him correct it as he completed each page," Lee pleasantly replied.

"Yeah, but I think it would be better if she helped me study for the math test. I got to pass that test, and we only got a few days. I can work on my essay at home tonight and bring it back tomorrow," Howard suggested.

"Now, Howard! You and I both know that you won't give that composition a minute's thought once you get home this evening. Lee can help you study your math this afternoon. I'm sure she'll see that you get lots of help with math before the test. She wants you to pass as much as I do. Don't you, Lee?" Miss Thompson asked.

"Maybe not quite as much as you, but I think it's very important that we all work hard and do our best," Lee replied.

"You see, Howard? Lee is totally committed to your success," Miss Thompson said as she gave him a hasty pat on the back.

"I don't think that's what she was saying. She . . ."

"Get busy on that composition, Howard," Miss Thompson ordered, interrupting his argument as she walked toward the next desk.

"You could at least help me get started," he appealed to Lee.

"I'm not going to help you with anything until you keep

your word. Now start writing," she said, pointing toward
his paper.

Lee beamed in triumph when Howard finally picked up
his pencil and began to write. But the moment was short-
lived. Her feelings of victory soon turned to pity as she
watched Howard struggle to set each word on paper. She
tried not to gawk, but it was hard to believe that someone
Howard's age was having such difficulty. He had written only
a few puzzling words by the time Miss Thompson dismissed
them for lunch.

"Don't look at me like that," he mumbled once Miss
Thompson was out of earshot.

"Like what?"

"Like I'm stupid or something," he fumed. "I know that's
what you're thinking."

"So you can read my mind, can you? Well, tell me what I'm
thinking right now, Howard," Lee challenged.

"Naw, I ain't so stupid as you think. You'd say I was wrong
no matter what I said," he crowed.

"I don't think you're stupid, but you do need to spend
more time on your schoolwork so you can pass your tests.
And I'm just the person to help you—if I get my teacup. So
where is it?"

Lee turned and watched as Howard ambled to the back of
the room. He walked into the cloakroom and a moment later
walked back toward her desk with his lunch pail. Placing his
fingers along the edge of the lid, he slowly pried it off. Lee
watched his hand dip into the bucket and scoop out a worn,
dirty rag. She held her breath as Howard placed it on the
desk. The soiled cloth fell away, revealing the delicate beauty
of her hand-painted teacup.

"Thank you, Howard," she said, reaching toward the cup.

With the speed of lightning, his hand shot forward and
grasped her wrist in a vise-like grip. "Just remember your end
of the bargain," he warned in a menacing voice. "I better pass

my tests, or I'll get that cup back and smash it to smithereens. You understand?"

"I understand, Howard. But you remember that I can't take the test for you. If you intend to pass, you'll have to study and do your lessons."

"Lee! Are you coming outside?" Lizzy called from the doorway.

"In a minute," she replied. "If you want to work on your essay during lunchtime or study your math, I'll stay inside and help you," Lee offered as she turned back toward Howard.

"I guess I better," he answered, giving her a lopsided grin.

She nodded. "I'm going to stay here and help Howard," Lee called to Lizzy, who remained at the doorway.

"You sure?" Lizzy asked in a puzzled voice.

"I'm sure," she replied, lifting the teacup.

Lizzy's face brightened into an enormous smile. "You still need to eat your lunch," her friend advised.

"You can go play, Lizzy. I'll get it for her," Howard stubbornly replied. "I'll write while you eat. As soon as you get done eating, we'll work on math. I promise I'll work on my essay tonight. I just gotta pass that math exam," he said, his fingers instinctively moving toward his blackened eye.

"Will your pa do that again if you don't pass?" Lee asked, nodding toward his eye.

"That's what he promised, and my pa keeps his promises— at least the ones I wish he'd forget."

"You'll pass, Howard. I promise," Lee said.

She sat beside him, quietly eating her lunch while he continued struggling to construct one sentence after another. As soon as she finished eating, Lee took out her slate and carefully wrote several rows of arithmetic problems. "Let's trade. You can begin working on this while I read your composition," she said while handing him the slate. Howard rewarded her with a bright smile and quickly set to work solving the problems until the rest of the class returned from lunch.

"You want to use this so your cup don't get broken on the way home?" Howard asked as the two of them prepared to leave school that afternoon. He shoved the dirty cloth into her hand.

"Thank you. I'll bring it back tomorrow," Lee said. She really didn't want to cover her beautiful teacup with the grimy rag, but she had no choice. Howard stood watching until she encased the teacup in the cloth and carefully placed it in her lunch pail.

"I'll be working on my composition tonight," he called out as their wagon began to pull away from the school.

"Looks like you got Howard eating out of your hand," Lizzy giggled. "Don't think I've ever seen that boy so agreeable."

"His pa beat him, Lizzy. That's why he has that swollen eye," Lee confided. "If he doesn't pass to the next grade, his pa vowed to whip him again. So I promised Howard that he'd pass."

"How you gonna guarantee such a thing? Ain't you that makes the decision on whether someone passes or fails," Lizzy chided.

"Miss Thompson said he'd pass if he does well on his tests and writes a good essay."

"He'll never be able to do that. That boy is dumb as a stump," Ben chortled from the front seat.

"That'll do, Ben," John chided. "You keep talking like that, and I'm gonna have to tell Pa you need a few lessons in proper manners. Don't reckon you want me doing that, do you?"

"Ain't doing nothing but telling the truth," Ben argued.

"I don't think he's dumb. Once he truly understands how to do something, he does fine. He got all his math correct after I spent some time with him. I think he'd rather not do his work, than do it wrong and be laughed at," Lee surmised.

"I don't know. He doesn't seem to have a problem laughing at other people and making them feel bad," Lizzy replied.

"That's true enough," Lee said, remembering some of the

hateful words he had directed at her only days earlier. "But maybe he'll change. Maybe if his pa quits hitting him, he'll be nicer to other people."

"We can only hope," John chimed in from the front of the wagon.

"And pray," Lee added, beginning to wonder if she'd made a terrible mistake promising Howard that he would be passed to the next grade. After all, it was Miss Thompson who would make the decision. Lee could help him, but she couldn't take the test or write his essay for him. Maybe Lizzy was right: she should have kept her mouth shut. Too late now. *Howard's not about to let me go back on my word*, she thought.

Chapter Ten

"Wonder what Pa and Fong are doing? They're usually down at the diggings," John remarked as he pulled back on the reins, signaling the mules to stop. There was an edge to his voice that caused Lee to peek around the side of the wagon to gain a better view.

The two men and Mrs. Smith appeared to be in a deep discussion. Fong's arms were waving in the air like a giant windmill, and Mr. Smith's face was etched with deep, angry lines. Mrs. Smith stood shaking her head back and forth while dabbing tears with her long, checkered apron.

What could be wrong? Lee felt her heart begin to pound. None of them moved from the wagon. They all sat there in frozen silence. Lee didn't know how long the four of them had been watching before Mrs. Smith looked in their direction and then nudged her husband. Three sets of eyes turned toward the wagon.

"What's wrong, Pa?" Ben called out.

"You children get on down and come inside," Mr. Smith ordered.

"He sounds real mad. You do something, Ben?" Lizzy accused.

"No. At least nothing comes to mind right off," he replied, a worried look crossing his face. A moment later he jerked around toward his sister. "I did rip my good pants last Sunday," he confessed.

Lizzy erupted in uneasy laughter at her brother's admission. "I don't think a pair of ripped pants would cause this much commotion," she replied as they walked toward the house.

"What do you think is wrong, John?" Lee asked, unable to squelch the fear that was rising up inside her like a fiery volcano.

"Only one way to find out," he replied while lifting her from the wagon before striding toward the cabin.

"What's wrong, Mama? Did you get some bad news?" Lizzy asked in a trembling voice.

Lee looked toward Fong, hoping he would give her a sign that everything was all right, but her brother's walnut brown eyes stared back at her and betrayed nothing. The air in the cabin was stale and heavy, adding to a sense of uneasiness in the room. Lee attempted a feeble smile, but it seemed to go unnoticed by the three adults.

"Ain't gonna waste a lot of time beating around the bush. We got us a real problem, and I expect the truth from all four of you," Mr. Smith firmly told them. "Don't expect no lying from any of you, or you'll just get in more trouble."

"What's going on, Pa?" John asked.

"Our gold's missing," Mr. Smith sternly replied. "You four younguns know anything about that?"

"What gold?" Lee meekly questioned. "I didn't know we had any gold," she continued, once again looking toward her brother for some sort of guidance.

Mr. Smith looked toward Fong. "I told her nothing. It is not our custom to trust girls with such information. She did not know about the gold," Fong confidently assured Mr. Smith.

"What about the rest of you?" he questioned, looking directly at his three children. "You better tell me now, before I go to the sheriff."

All three of the children stared wide-eyed at their father. "Don't know anything about it," John finally answered, while Lizzy and Ben nodded their heads in agreement. "We'd never steal from our own family," John continued. "You and Ma have taught us better than that, Pa."

Mr. Smith lowered his head until Lee thought that it would

touch his broad chest. "I guess I'm just grasping at straws, hoping there's some easy answer. I don't want to believe that our gold has been stolen. All that hard work—I don't see how we can keep on ..."

"Now, Silas, don't be talking like that in front of the children," Mrs. Smith interrupted. "Lizzy, you and Lee get started on your schoolwork. John, take your brother and chop some firewood—it's getting low," she instructed. "Come on, Silas. Let's go outside to finish this discussion," she urged, taking her husband's hand and leading him toward the doorway.

Lee watched Fong follow behind Mr. and Mrs. Smith and soon heard their muted conversation drifting through the open windows as she and Lizzy opened their books. "Things ain't sounding too good," Lizzy said, breaking the deadly silence that filled the room. "If all our gold is gone, I don't know what's gonna happen. Just last week, Ma said we was getting low on supplies."

"Maybe Fong has some of our money left. I'll talk to him and see," Lee suggested. "Did they find a lot of gold?"

"Pa said something about some big nuggets and seemed to be real excited when he was talking to Ma a couple of weeks ago. I didn't pay much attention, but he did say we'd be sitting pretty if it didn't peter out too soon," Lizzy confided.

"What does that mean—'sitting pretty if it doesn't peter out'?" Lee asked. Mrs. Conroy had an uncle named Peter; then there was Peter in the Bible. But what did that have to do with 'peter out'? And who decided what was considered 'sitting pretty'? Did it mean your dress was fluffed out around you and your legs were crossed just right? And what did how you were sitting have to do with Peter? What a confusing remark!

Lizzy giggled at her friend's obvious puzzlement. "Sitting pretty means that we'd have enough money not to worry about buying supplies. And petered out means the same as running out of something. Pa meant we'd have enough gold to take care of us if they found a little more before it ran out."

Lee's look of bewilderment faded. "Did you know where they had the gold hidden?" she asked.

"No, of course not. Pa probably would have told me if I had asked," she quickly added. "But I never had no need to know—never even thought about it."

"We have to find it," Lee replied.

"Don't know how we'd ever find it. Maybe if we talk to John, he'll have an idea," Lizzy suggested.

"Or Howard O'Laughlin," Lee replied.

"Howard O'Laughlin? Why would you want to ask him?"

Lee couldn't help but laugh at Lizzy's astounded look. "I think Howard's probably had some experience trying to solve problems like this," Lee answered. "Besides, it couldn't hurt to get some advice from him."

"Never thought I'd see the day when I thought Howard O'Laughlin could give me any sound advice," Lizzy replied. "Maybe it's not such a bad idea, but tell him to keep his mouth shut," she cautioned.

"I'll talk to him tomorrow."

"What you two gabbing about?" John asked, carrying in an armload of wood and placing it in a box beside the fireplace.

"Trying to figure out who took the gold and what's gonna happen to us," Lizzy replied.

"I sure can't figure it out. Don't know how anybody would have known where to find it buried out there."

"Buried out where?" Lizzy asked. "Why was it buried?"

"Pa buried it below that big black oak out behind the cabin. They didn't want to keep the gold inside the house— figured if we was all gone, that would be the first place a thief would look. Guess he and Fong agreed it would be best to bury it. Each evening, they added the day's find to what was already buried—at least that's what they used to do."

"Show us where it was," Lizzy begged, jumping up from the table.

"Oh, yes, please show us," Lee begged.

Their eyes grew large as John took them to the base of the large old oak tree. A pile of dried leaves and acorns had been pushed aside, and the secret hiding place was now nothing more than a yawning hole in the moist dirt. It was hard to believe someone could have discovered such an unlikely hiding place, but someone had. And now their lives hung in the balance. How could they afford to remain in Striker's Gulch if they had no money for supplies? Yet how could they afford to leave?

A deafening silence filled the cabin as they ate their evening meal. Only moments earlier, Mr. Smith had seemed to have difficulty finding the words to give thanks for their food. When Fong left the cabin after dinner, Lee hobbled along after him. "I want to talk to you," she said as they entered the small clearing in front of the cabin, "about our money."

His head snapped up. "What money?"

"The money we brought from China. Is there nothing left?"

"No. I had hidden it with the gold," he said. "Not so smart," he added, shaking his head sadly.

"You didn't think it would be stolen," Lee replied, hoping she could comfort him.

"That's just it, I didn't think. Go back inside and help with the dishes. There's nothing left to talk about. Mr. Smith and I will decide what must be done," he said, dismissing her.

The next morning the four children left for school as they did every other weekday morning. But this time it was different. A sense of gloom seemed to overshadow them. When Howard presented Lee with several pages of his composition, she merely nodded and said that she would read them later. Even Miss Thompson's jovial announcement that there would be a ceremony and party for all students being promoted to the next grade did little to brighten Lee's spirits.

"What's wrong with you?" Howard asked as they began to

98

work on his essay during recess. "You act like you lost your best friend or something."

"Can you keep a secret?" Lee asked in a hushed voice as she turned to make sure no one was around.

"Of course I can. What's going on?"

"Our gold was stolen, and if we don't get it back, we won't even have enough money to buy supplies," Lee confided. "I thought you might have some idea how we could catch whoever did it," Lee continued, sounding more hopeful than she felt.

"I might. How did it happen?"

"The gold was in a tin buried out under a big tree a short distance from the house. I think it must have happened a couple of nights ago. My brother discovered that it was missing yesterday afternoon."

Howard nodded his head and seemed to be deep in thought. "Did John know you were going to tell me?" Howard asked after several minutes had passed.

"Yes. But I'm not sure he thought it was such a good idea," she honestly replied.

"I don't doubt that. We'll talk again after school. I think I might be able to help out," he explained. "Have you read my paper yet?" he asked, pointing toward the essay lying unnoticed on her desk.

"I'll read it now," Lee said, giving him a paltry smile as she picked up the paper and began reviewing his work. Surprisingly, it was much better than Lee had anticipated. Overall, it was a well-written theme outlining a variety of methods used for trapping animals. Although Lee found the subject somewhat disgusting, Howard had followed her advice and written about a topic with which he was well acquainted.

"Well?" he asked when she reached the end of the essay and finally lifted her head. He was obviously anxious to hear her remarks.

"It's very good, Howard. You did a fine job. After we discuss a few corrections, you can make the changes tonight and tell Miss Thompson you're prepared to read it in class," Lee praised. "I feel certain you'll get a good grade." She was relieved that Howard had been true to his word and prepared the essay. It was obvious he was capable of doing his lessons. So why hadn't he just done his best work to start with? She might never understand Howard O'Laughlin, but at least he had written a good essay. Now if he could just pass the math test!

Chapter Eleven

Lee's kind remarks caused Howard's cheeks to blush until they matched his flaming red hair. His hand moved toward his rosy face, and he turned and looked out the window.

"How come you're nice to me?" he asked, still looking away. "I figured as soon as you got your teacup back, you wouldn't teach me. I know Miss Thompson said you had to, but I thought you'd just make out like you was helping and let me fail. How come you never told Miss Thompson I took your teacup? And I know you ain't afraid of me, so my threats didn't have nothing to do with it," he hastily added, finally turning back to meet her gaze.

"I did have some unkind thoughts about helping you when Miss Thompson first gave me the assignment," Lee replied with a giggle. "But I gave you my word that I would help you if you returned my teacup."

"You could have kept your word without being nice to me," he interjected.

"That's true! And there were times when it was hard to be nice to you. But when I was thoughtful, you finally began treating me better. After my parents' death several years ago, I lived with Christian missionaries in Canton—Mr. and Mrs. Conroy. They were wonderful people. Mrs. Conroy taught me how to read and write, but she also taught me about the love of God. One of the last things she told me before I sailed for America was to return kindness for unkindness. I've learned that's a very hard thing to do."

Howard listened intently. "I'm not so sure that works all the time—that stuff about being kind."

"Maybe not, but it's better than being hateful. When I say and do mean things, I feel bad down inside," Lee replied, pointing toward her heart. "How come you were so mean to me, Howard? Did I do something that made you want to hurt me, or was it just because I look different?" Lee asked cautiously.

Howard stared at her thoughtfully. "I guess it's just the way I am. I make fun of people."

"But why?" Lee asked, still unable to understand.

"So they don't get a chance to make fun of me first. I got this red hair and all these freckles and this here space 'tween my teeth," he explained, pointing from his hair to his freckles to his teeth. "I ain't what you'd call handsome. In fact, my pa says I'm plug-ugly and as worthless as the day is long. Guess that's true enough," he added, giving her a halfhearted smile.

"Nobody is ugly or worthless in God's eyes, Howard. He created each of us to look different. Mr. Smith says he thinks God likes variety. I think so too," Lee said, returning Howard's smile.

"Maybe. But I'd rather look like Bill or Charlie so nobody would notice me. With this red hair and freckles, ain't no way to hide. I remember my first day of school when we was living back in New York. All them kids laughing and pointing, calling me tomato-head and snaggle tooth—made up my mind right then, I wasn't gonna let people treat me that way."

Lee stared into Howard's glazed eyes. He looked as though he had returned to the school in New York and was once again being ridiculed—the class scapegoat. Sadly, it seemed their unkind bantering and jokes had turned Howard into the class bully.

"So what did you do?" Lee asked.

"I learned to fight. Got my share of bloody noses and black eyes, but pretty soon, I was winning. That's when they quit calling me names—when I could win the fights."

"And did they become your friends?"

"Naw. They still didn't want anything to do with the likes

of me, but at least they left me alone. I hated going to that class, but my pa was bent on getting me schooled. Said he expected me to become more than a potato farmer. I was so glad when he told me we was moving to California. I was even happier when we got here and there weren't no school. But more and more people came, and pretty soon the folks wanted a school. When my pa said I'd be going back to school, I made up my mind right then and there that nobody would make fun of me," Howard explained.

"Don't you see how that works, Howard? Those kids were mean to you, and you began treating others the same way. But that's also how it works if you're friendly. I was kind to you, and now you're nice to me. Sometimes it takes a while before folks return kindness, but I still think it's a better way," Lee replied.

"So is that why you kept telling me Jesus loved me when I was mean to you?"

Lee smiled and looked away for a moment. "I'm ashamed to admit this, but when I told you that Jesus loved you, those were the only kind words I could manage to get out of my mouth. You were so hateful to me. I didn't want to treat you badly, so I said the only truth I could find in my heart—that Jesus loves you."

"Do you really believe that Jesus loves me?" Howard asked.

"I know that Jesus loves you, Howard. He may not love the things you do or the way you sometimes act, but He loves you," Lee vowed.

The clatter of feet and chattering voices interrupted their discussion as the rest of the children began to return from the lunch recess. "How's the arithmetic coming along?" Miss Thompson inquired as she walked to the front of the class-room. "I thought we might take the test tomorrow. How does that sound?"

Howard couldn't pass the test just yet since he still hadn't mastered the division problems. Lee was angry with herself for talking through their lunchtime instead of helping Howard with his assignment. Her mind was racing, and butterflies were banging around in her stomach again. She hated that feeling. "It doesn't sound like a very good idea," she ventured while giving Miss Thompson her sweetest smile.

"And why not? We have only two weeks of school left before the end of the year. It's not wise to put things off until the last minute. I'll need time to grade the tests, you know."

"Yes, ma'am. I wouldn't ask, but I had planned on helping Howard with his division during lunch recess . . ."

"And?" Miss Thompson interrupted.

"It's my fault. I started talking to Howard about other things, so we didn't get to his arithmetic. It wouldn't be fair if he failed the test because I spent our study time talking," Lee claimed.

"What about your essay, Howard? Can you be prepared to read it in class tomorrow?"

"Yes, Ma'am," he proudly replied. "I'll be ready."

"That's what we'll do then. You read your essay tomorrow, but be prepared to take the test next Monday," Miss Thompson replied. "And no excuses," she added, looking at both of them.

"No excuses," they agreed in unison.

That gave them lunchtime tomorrow to practice. However, Lee wasn't sure that would be enough time to get Howard ready. "I don't think I'm going to pass," Howard said, as if reading her mind.

Lee thought for a few moments. "Can you come to church? There's a basket dinner afterward, and everyone stays and visits all afternoon. I could help you then."

"Oh, that's not fair. Everyone else will be having fun, but you'll be stuck doing lessons with me."

Howard's thoughtfulness surprised Lee. Maybe he was beginning to understand. "It's all right, Howard. All the others go off and play games. I can't join in," she said, nodding toward her feet. "You'll be good company. Please say you'll come," she urged.

"I don't know. Folks at church probably wouldn't want me there," Howard said, hanging his head.

"Why do you think that?" Lee asked.

"One time I heard Mrs. Conklin say that I was a little heathen. Mrs. Johnson agreed with her and said the church would probably cave in if I ever darkened the doorway."

"But they were joking, Howard," Lee replied.

"Maybe, maybe not. Folks don't like me, and I know it," Howard said while keeping his head lowered.

"Why don't you give it a chance? If people don't treat you right, you don't have to come back. How about that?" Lee reasoned.

"I'll ask my ma. If she says it's okay, I'll be there," he agreed.

Lee spotted Lizzy at the back of the classroom waiting for her when classes ended that afternoon. *Lizzy's never going to believe that Howard's coming to church,* Lee thought. She couldn't wait to tell her.

"I'll walk you out to the wagon," Howard offered. "Unless you want me to carry you?"

"I can walk. But thanks anyway," Lee replied, politely dismissing him. But even when Lizzy joined them, Howard continued to walk slowly beside her. She'd have to wait until they were on their way home to tell Lizzy the news.

When the trio reached the wagon, Howard scooped Lee into his arms and deposited her in the back of the wagon. John and Ben looked stunned, but neither said a word. Their mouths fell open when he turned and lifted Lizzy and placed her beside Lee. "Any luck catching that thief?" he asked, looking toward John.

"What? Oh, the thief, no—no luck yet," John stammered, attempting to hide his amazement.

"Maybe you didn't get the snare set just right. Want me to come over and take a look see? I wouldn't mind," he offered.

"Thanks for asking, but I ain't told my pa, and he might get suspicious if he sees us out there fooling around. We been checking for broken twigs and signs that anyone's been coming around, but so far it don't look like he's been back," John said.

"Sure hope you get him," Howard replied. "See ya tomorrow."

"Yeah, see ya," John replied, pulling his straw hat down over his forehead to shade his eyes from the hot afternoon sun. "Can't believe the change in that boy," John commented. "Hard to believe he's the same person."

"Guess what?" Lee whispered in Lizzy's ear.

"What?"

"I think Howard's going to come to church on Sunday. He said he'd ask his ma, and if she said it was all right, he'd be there."

"You're joking me," Lizzy chortled until she saw that Lee wasn't laughing with her. "For sure? He said he would come to church?"

Lee nodded. "I promised to help him with his arithmetic after the basket lunch. You think your mama would mind fixing enough to feed one more person?"

"Supplies are kind of short right now, but I know Ma would do without anything to eat if it meant getting somebody else to attend church."

"That's what I thought, too. Your folks are a lot like the Conroys. They want everybody to know Jesus."

Lizzy nodded her head in agreement. "Pa's been talking to Fong, trying to get him to understand about God's love for him."

"How do you know that?" Lee asked.

"I heard my folks talking about it the other night. Seems things was going real good, too—until the gold was stolen. I guess your brother told Pa that if God loved us so much, He shouldn't have let that happen," Lizzy said.

"He can't blame that on God," Lee protested.

"Maybe you don't think that way, but that doesn't change what your brother thinks," Lizzy replied. "Never know, he may change his mind. We'll have to keep praying for him. So far God's been answering our prayers. Look what's happened to Howard. If he can change, anybody can."

Lee nodded her head. If only Fong would open up his heart a little bit, she knew that God would rush in.

Chapter Twelve

It was after midnight when a thundering ruckus awakened the entire household. Lee and Lizzy watched in fear as Mr. Smith grabbed his shotgun from above the fireplace and headed for the door, with Fong following close behind. The revolver he had purchased in Chinatown was shaking in one hand, and an unlit lantern dangled from the other. Lee hoped he wouldn't accidentally shoot Mr. Smith. After all, her brother had never owned such a weapon before.

"Wish we could go out and see," Lizzy murmured excitedly.

"Hope we finally caught what we were after," John replied in a hushed voice as he came down from the loft.

"What are you children whispering about?" Mrs. Smith asked.

"John! Come out here and help us!" Mr. Smith yelled, trying to make himself heard over all the commotion. In his excitement Fong was yelling in Chinese, but there was another voice screaming curses into the night air.

"Well, look what we got here," John called out while approaching a man hanging upside down by his ankles from a stout tree branch. The man was wiggling around like bacon frying in a skillet. "Better quit your squirming or you're liable to fall on your head," John warned.

"What do you know about this?" Silas asked his son, holding the lantern high to gain a better view of the spectacle.

"We set a trap to see if the culprit who stole the gold would come back," John quietly informed his father. "I think we should have a talk before you cut him down."

"Where you going?" the man yelled in a panic-filled voice

as John, Silas, and Fong moved closer to the cabin to begin their discussion.

"Just hold your horses. We'll be back," Silas called to him.

"All the blood's rushing to my head, and I'm gonna pass out if you don't get me down from here," the man called after them.

"Well if you do faint, things will be a lot quieter around here. Besides, you got yourself into this mess," Silas replied. "Now, what's going on?" he asked, turning toward John.

"We set a trap hoping the thief would come back. Each evening I would go out under the tree and act like I was putting gold in the ground, hoping he was watching and would try to steal from us again. We set up a snare, so I had to be careful not to trip it when I went out there each evening," John explained. "We were beginning to think the bandit was long gone. We almost gave up."

"We? Who else was in on this?" Mr. Smith asked, glancing over his shoulder at the spectacle hanging from the tree.

"Ben, Lizzy, Lee, and Howard O'Laughlin," John answered.

"Howard O'Laughlin? How in the world did he get involved in this? From what I know about that boy, I'd come closer to thinking he stole our money than helped us recover it," Mr. Smith remarked.

"It was Lee's idea. She was assigned to help him with his schoolwork and figured he might know how to go about catching a polecat like him," John said, pointing toward the man.

"I guess he did. Well, we better get this feller down and see what he has to say for himself," Silas replied. "You want to crawl up that tree and cut him down?" he asked John as they walked back toward where the man was hanging.

"I'll do it," Fong replied, quickly grabbing hold of a lower branch and shinnying up the tree trunk. After pulling a knife from the leather sheath attached to his belt, Fong began to methodically saw at the rope.

"I'm gonna fall on my head if he cuts me loose like that," the man called down toward Silas and John.

"Might knock some sense into you," John retorted.

"We'll do our best to break your fall," Silas told the man. "Can't do much more than that," he added, just as the man came tumbling from the tree. John and Silas grabbed him and managed to deflect his landing enough to prevent any major injuries. But his feet had no more than touched the ground then the rascal jumped up and began to scurry off into the shadowy darkness. Fong lurched forward with the speed of lightning and extended his leg as the culprit ran by, once again sending the man toppling to the ground. Silas soon tied the man's hands behind his back and pushed him along until they returned to the front of the cabin.

"Who are you, anyway?" Silas asked. "Ain't never seen you in these parts."

"Abe Johnson," the scraggly man answered. "And I been around here longer than most of you gold diggers."

"You got some explaining to do, and I suggest you begin right now," Mr. Smith commanded.

"I was out for a stroll and got caught up in your snare," the man replied. "Ain't no law against takin' a walk through the woods, now is there?"

"Nope, ain't no law about that. But there is a law against stealing. How come you got a hole dug up under the tree out yonder if you was just taking a stroll?" John asked.

"Didn't steal nothing. Weren't nothing out there to steal," he answered, giving John an evil grin.

"Don't reckon you'd mind if we take a look in your knapsack?" Mr. Smith asked, producing the dirty bag that Fong had discovered nearby.

"Give me that! You keep your dirty hands off my belongings," Abe screamed. "You ain't got my permission to look in there."

"Well, that makes us even. I didn't give you permission to get into my belongings, either," Mr. Smith replied while untying the leather laces and dumping the contents onto the ground.

"Whoa! Look at that," Ben croaked.

It was several moments before anybody spoke. "Don't nobody touch any of that. It's mine!" Abe Johnson hollered. "Get away from there," he hissed at Fong, who was bent down sorting through the pile of gold and silver.

"This yours too?" Fong asked as he held a coin in front of the man's face.

"Everything in there's mine. I found it all, fair and square."

"Where did you find this?" Fong asked, continuing to wave the coin in front of Mr. Johnson.

"I don't remember. Probably got it in San Francisco," he hedged.

Fong pulled several other coins from the mound. "These all belonged to my family. I brought them from China. And these," he continued, holding up several pieces, "are gold nuggets you stole from us."

"Ain't no way you can prove that," Abe said, giving a wicked laugh. "Gold is gold. Ain't no way you can prove it's yours."

Fong pointed to a small mark carved in each of the nuggets he held. "We marked our nuggets."

"And these pouches belong to us," Mr. Smith shouted, holding up two leather pouches that carried the same mark. "I just wonder who you stole the rest of this from. John, get some more rope. We'll tie him to the wagon wheel until morning. Then I think we'd better pay a visit to the sheriff."

"Now, hold up. You got your gold back, and I'm willing to split the rest of my loot," Mr. Johnson offered. "That's a mighty good deal. You'd be fools to turn down an offer like that."

"Well I guess we're fools, but we don't believe in keeping things that don't belong to us. You stole from people who are working hard just to eke out a living. That ain't right. If you want gold, you should be out here working for it, like the rest of us. We're not about to set you free," Mr. Smith lectured as he secured the ropes around the wagon wheel. "You might as well settle down and get some sleep—that's what I plan to do," he told the thief. "Come along," he said, motioning to the rest of them. "There's still time to get a little sleep before morning."

The next day, Abe Johnson was exactly where they'd left him the night before, tied to the wagon wheel and still complaining. They climbed into the wagon, the adults up front and all of the children in the back along with Abe Johnson, who was trussed up like a pig going to market.

"You take the wagon on over to school," Mr. Smith told John as he came to a halt in front of the makeshift jail. "Your ma's got shopping to do, and we need to talk to the sheriff. Think we'll stay in town and relax a bit—might even take your ma over to that new boardinghouse for lunch."

"I could ask Iris Crane's pa to give us a ride," John said.

"No, this will be fine. Don't think any of us are going to mind a day away from work. Get along now," he said, grabbing Abe by the arm and leading him toward the jail.

Lee watched Fong and Mr. Smith walk into the jail. Mrs. Smith was heading down the dusty street toward the general store, her head held high and a large basket swinging from her arm. With their gold recovered, it was obvious that she was going to enjoy her grocery shopping today.

"Won't be any problem having enough food for the basket dinner on Sunday," Lizzy commented as they continued off toward the school.

Howard was waiting in the schoolyard when they arrived. As soon as the wagon came to a halt, he rushed to the rear of the wagon and lifted both girls out. "My ma says I can come on Sunday," he announced enthusiastically.

"Come where?" Ben asked, jumping from the front seat.

"To church. Lee asked me," he said, giving them a grin. "Is something wrong?" he asked when John and Ben stared at him dumbfounded.

"No, nothing wrong. Just surprised—ain't never seen you at church," John answered as soon as he could finally get his tongue working.

"That's 'cause I ain't never been there. Gotta be a first time for everything—leastwise that's what my ma says."

"That's true enough. Say, we got some news for you, too," John said as they began walking toward the school. "We caught our thief last night. That snare of yours worked finer than frog's hair!"

"Who was it? Did you get your gold back? Where is he?" Howard fired off his questions in rapid succession while excitedly hopping from foot to foot. "Tell me everything."

"Later," John answered. "The bell's ringing. We'd better get inside."

They had hardly gotten in their seats when Miss Thompson called Howard to the front of the room to read his essay. "Wish me luck," he whispered to Lee.

"I'll do better than that. I'll say a prayer," Lee replied. She could tell he was nervous. His voice squeaked and his cheeks had turned a rosy shade of red. Several boys in the back of the room snickered, and Lee could see him stiffen. He needed to relax and ignore those boys! Lee pretended to cough, and Howard glanced in her direction. She gave him an encouraging smile and hoped it would be enough to divert his attention from the rowdy boys who wanted him to fail. It worked. He cleared his throat and in a steady voice began to read, his gaze never wandering back to those boys.

"That was very, very good, Howard—an excellent recitation. I am very impressed," Miss Thompson commended.

Howard beamed at Lee as he returned to his seat. "She liked it," he whispered with a look of astonishment on his face.

"I told you it was good," Lee whispered back. "You did a wonderful job reading it, too."

"Thanks. Miss Thompson?" Howard called out, raising his hand.

"Yes, Howard?"

"Could I say something else?"

"Yes, of course," she replied. "What is it?"

Howard stood up and turned toward the class. "I just want all of you to know that I think Lee is the smartest student in this school—maybe in the whole county. If it weren't for her help these past weeks, I would have failed all my tests. Ain't no way I could have written such a fine essay without her help." He looked back toward Miss Thompson. "That's all I got to say, Ma'am."

"That was very nice, Howard. I'm pleased that you appreciate Lee's help, and I'm sure she appreciates your kind words," Miss Thompson replied. "Don't forget—you still have that arithmetic test on Monday," she added.

"Yes, Ma'am. And I plan to pass that one, too," Howard answered obediently. However, he had barely uttered his answer when several boys sitting at the back of the room began hooting and calling him a sissy. His face flamed bright red, and he suddenly swung around in the desk, his fists clenched in anger.

"Just ignore them," Lee whispered, touching his arm. "Remember, it's kindness that works."

Howard nodded his head. "It would be more fun to box their ears, but I'll do it your way," he said. "Who knows? Maybe it will work."

Lee peered longingly toward the door when lunchtime arrived. The beautiful spring day seemed to beckon her outdoors to enjoy the warm breeze and singing birds.

"You wish you could be out there with Lizzy, don't you?" Howard asked. Sometimes she thought he could read her mind. "Why don't we go out there and eat? Then we can come back inside when they start playing," he suggested.

Lee nodded in agreement, her eyes sparkling with anticipation. It seemed like forever since she'd gotten to sit on the steps and enjoy the sunshine while eating lunch and talking with her friend. Howard didn't ask permission; he just gathered her into his arms and carried her out to the front porch and sat her on the top step.

"Lee!" Lizzy shouted, running from the schoolyard and up the steps. "Aren't you and Howard studying today?" she asked.

"We're going to eat outside. We'll go back and study after we finish lunch." The two girls began nibbling on the big, fluffy biscuits that Mrs. Smith had tucked into their lunch pails. "Looks like John and Ben are telling Howard all about last night," Lee said, pointing toward where the three boys stood huddled together.

"Hard to believe there's been such a change in Howard. I never thought there was any hope for that boy, but you sure enough changed that," Lizzy commented as she watched her brothers laughing with their new friend. Nearby, a lone wood-pecker hammered into the side of a towering black oak, its rat-a-tat-tat mingling with the boys' laughter.

"He's a different person, that's for sure," Lee agreed as she motioned for Howard to join her. "Wish I could stay out here and visit, but we've got little time and lots of work before Howard can pass that test."

"You think he can do it? You've worked so hard helping him that I sure hope he passes."

Lizzy's look of concern warmed Lee's heart. "If he doesn't pass, I'm afraid he'll go back to his old ways, and I don't want that to happen. I don't want his pa using a strap on him anymore, either. It's going to take a lot of work and a lot of prayer," Lee answered.

"I can sure help out with the praying part—John and Ben, too. Why, I'm sure I could even get Ma and Pa to pray for him," Lizzy offered, her face lighting up with excitement.

"What you two busy planning?" Howard asked as he approached the two girls. He took two giant steps and flopped down beside them on the small porch.

"No need getting comfortable. It's time to get busy on

arithmetic," Lee sternly admonished, trying to suppress a smile.

"She ain't half as mean as she lets on," Howard said to Lizzy. "She just wants folks to think she's tough," he continued, giving an exaggerated wink. Lee couldn't keep a straight face, and both girls immediately burst into rippling laughter.

"That's enough! 'It's time to get busy on arithmetic,'" Howard mimicked. "You want to walk or ride piggyback?" Howard asked while stooping down for Lee to hop on his back.

"I think I'll walk. It's probably safer," she replied before giving him a broad smile.

"I'm glad you got your gold back," Howard said, once they had returned to their desk.

"If it weren't for you, we never would have caught him," Lee replied.

Howard's face turned crimson; his embarrassment was obvious. "Naw, you would have found a way without me. John or Ben would have come up with an idea."

"Don't go selling yourself short, Howard," Miss Thompson said as she walked into the room. "John told me what happened last night. I think you played an important part in the capture of that villain. You should be proud of yourself; I know I am. I'm very pleased with the changes I see taking place in your life, Howard. You just keep up the good work," Miss Thompson said as she gave him a pat on the back.

Howard gave Lee a sheepish grin. "It's kind of nice to have folks thinking good about me for a change," he admitted. "'Course my pa still says I'm useless. The only thing that's gonna change his mind is if I pass to the next grade."

"Only one more test to go!" Lee encouraged as she tried to erase the haunting picture of Howard's battered face from her mind.

Chapter Thirteen

Promotion day finally arrived. Billowy marshmallow clouds floated through a sapphire blue sky, and a bright, golden sun provided just the right amount of warmth. Lizzy's eyes sparkled in delight, her pink-flowered muslin dress receiving applause from the family. John and Ben appeared quite handsome in their dark breeches and white shirts. Convinced by Mrs. Smith to wear traditional Chinese clothes, Lee wore a red satin skirt and jacket trimmed with white and blue embroidery; her hair was adorned with fancy combs that had belonged to her mother. Once the children had received Mrs. Smith's approval, they next received the explicit instructions that they had better not get dirty or snag their clothes before the big event.

"Ain't Ma never gonna get done in there?" Ben asked for the umpteenth time.

"Now don't be asking me that anymore," Mr. Smith chided. "It don't make things go any faster just because you keep whining."

"I ain't whining. Babies whine—I'm just asking," Ben quickly defended when he turned and saw the girls snickering at Mr. Smith's remark.

"I think I'm finally ready," Mrs. Smith said, fluttering out the front door in a blue print calico she'd finished stitching just the night before.

"My, my, don't you look nice," Mr. Smith said, giving her a broad smile. "That's a very pretty dress—and so is the lady wearing it." The children all chuckled as he bent from the waist, sweeping his arm across his body in a courtly bow.

"Your wagon awaits, my lady," he teased, helping her up onto the seat.

The deep green conifers, flowering redbuds, plum trees, and acacia all seemed to spring alive as the wagon passed by. Lee thought that she had never seen anything quite so lovely. The air was a perfumed mixture of damp moss and pungent wildflowers, and she inhaled deeply. It made her think of Mrs. Conroy. I'll write her a letter this evening and tell her every detail of the day's events, Lee thought, willing herself to remember every aspect of the promotion ceremonies.

"How come you're so quiet?" Lizzy whispered in Lee's ear.

"I was thinking about Mrs. Conroy. I'm going to write her a letter as soon as we get home. Will you help me remember everything that happens today? I don't want to forget to tell her anything," Lee replied.

"I'll try. Let's just hope that Howard passed his test so that all the news you write her is happy. I think she'll be mighty proud to know how much you were able to help him," Lizzy said, giving her friend a big smile.

It seemed as though only a few minutes had passed when Mr. Smith pulled the mules to a halt in the schoolyard. Jumping down, he helped Mrs. Smith while Fong lifted Lee out of the wagon.

"You boys jump on out of there and help your sister," Mr. Smith called out.

"I'm so excited I can hardly stand it," Lizzy reported as they climbed out of the wagon and moved toward the plank benches that had been set up in the schoolyard.

The outdoor ceremony had been Miss Thompson's idea. In case of bad weather, they were to move indoors, but it didn't appear that was going to be necessary. Lee glanced around the crowd, hoping to catch a glimpse of Howard and his parents. Miss Thompson refused to tell who would be promoted or receive special awards, explaining that she wanted all of her students and their parents to attend. The chairs and benches were rapidly being claimed.

Miss Thompson was strolling among the parents and children, attired in a pale gold linen dress with tiny green leaves embroidered on the collar and cuffs. Her chestnut brown hair was parted in the middle and fell into long, plump curls instead of the usual severe bun at the back of her head. Lee thought she looked lovely and told her so. Miss Thompson replied, "And I think your skirt and jacket are exquisite. You look very pretty in red."

Lee smiled. Mrs. Conroy used to tell her the same thing. "Thank you. In China, the colors red and gold represent happiness and good fortune. Today, I am very happy, and you must be too!" Lee said, pointing to Miss Thompson's dress.

"I wore a gold dress and didn't even realize that it meant happiness or good fortune. But now that I know, I'm certainly glad I made this choice," Miss Thompson remarked.

"Oh look, there's Howard. I was afraid he was going to be late," Lee said, pointing toward the battered wagon that was pulling into the schoolyard. "I hope he's going to pass," she said, giving Miss Thompson a doleful glance.

"You know I can't tell you, Lee. You'll know soon enough," she said while giving the girl an affectionate pat. "Excuse me. I want to greet some of the parents," she said, turning to survey the crowd.

Howard waved and gave Lee a big smile. He was wearing his usual coveralls, plaid shirt, and scuffed brown boots. His father's attire was much the same. Mrs. O'Laughlin was dressed in a brown homespun dress, and her head was covered with a braided straw hat, which was tied under her chin with a piece of frayed ribbon. Miss Thompson was talking to Howard's father; meanwhile, Howard and his mother were headed in Lee's direction.

"I wanted my ma to meet you," Howard said as they grew closer. "Ma, this here is Lee, the girl I went to church with."

"And the one who's been helping you with your schoolwork. I'm pleased to meet you, Lee," Mrs. O'Laughlin said. "Howard tells me you're a very good teacher. And you've had a wonderful influence on him," she added in a whisper.

"Howard! You and your ma get over here," Mr. O'Laughlin bellowed from across the schoolyard. His father's outburst had drawn the attention of everyone attending the festivities, and Howard's face instantly burned red with embarrassment. He promptly led his mother back to his father, who stood by the benches shoving a plug of tobacco into his cheek.

"Please find a seat so that we may begin. Students, please take your places in the front rows," Miss Thompson called from the makeshift stage that Mr. Crane, owner of the general store and Iris Crane's father, had constructed for their use. Earlier that week, the students had practiced the proper method for walking onto the stage and receiving their promotion diplomas from Miss Thompson.

"Hope all that practice wasn't for nothing," Howard said as he sat down beside Lee. "My pa said I was in big trouble if he came here for nothing. I sure wish Miss Thompson would have told us if we passed," he rambled nervously.

"It's going to be all right, Howard. You told me the test didn't seem all that hard," Lee reminded him.

"Yeah, but now that I think about it, I'm not so sure. I probably got a lot more wrong than I thought."

"Let's begin," Miss Thompson said, glancing out over the crowd. "First, let me say to the parents that I have enjoyed having your children as my students this year. I am pleased that you have chosen to attend our ceremonies today."

"Didn't have much choice," Mr. O'Laughlin remarked in a voice loud enough to be heard by the entire group.

Howard slouched down between Lee and John. Lee gave him a sympathetic smile. Miss Thompson chose to ignore the remark and continued her welcoming speech. Then she asked Mr. Sampson, the mayor of Striker's Gulch, to come to the stage and assist her with the diplomas. Howard held his breath as she methodically called out the names of the students, shook each one's hand, and passed each graduate along to Mr. Sampson. Once they received their certificates, the students lined up along the back of the stage. The names were called in alphabetical order, and Tommy Hill and Charles Mackey had been left sitting in their chairs.

"Mary Nelson," Miss Thompson called from the stage. Lee gave Howard's hand a squeeze. He would be next . . . if he was going to pass. They both sat frozen in their seats while staring directly at Miss Thompson's face, hoping that she would give them some sort of sign. Nothing. Mary walked slowly to the rear of the stage. Finally, Miss Thompson turned to once again face the audience. "Howard O'Laughlin," she called out clearly.

Lee gave his hand another squeeze and nudged him off the bench. "Get up there," she urged. "Go get your certificate."

Howard proudly walked to the stage and shook Miss Thompson's hand.

"Congratulations, Howard! Well done."

"Never thought I'd see the day," his father mumbled from several rows back while Mrs. O'Laughlin clapped wildly, her pride obvious for all to see.

Soon Lee, Lizzy, John, and Ben received their diplomas, together with most of the other students. There were a few who remained in their seats, and Lee felt a surge of pity for them even though most were the group of bullies that Howard used to associate with. She couldn't help but think that Howard might have been down there with them if things hadn't changed. The crowd gave the class a rousing round of applause before they returned to their assigned seats.

"We have another award to make this afternoon, and I'm going to ask Mr. Sampson to come forward and tell you about it," Miss Thompson announced. There was a buzz through the audience as Ernie Sampson made his way across the stage and stood before them.

"If you could quiet down now, I'd like to be sure everyone can hear what I've got to say," he called out. The group finally grew quiet. In fact, the only sound remaining was the twittering of birds singing to each other as they flew from tree to tree. "Some of you folks know there's been some trouble here in Striker's Gulch. We've had a thief among us," he announced. Once again a hum of voices spread through the crowd. "For those of you who didn't know, there's no need to get upset. The thief has been apprehended!" A roar of applause and cheers followed his announcement.

"It seems we had a thief who was moving up and down the river stealing from hard-working gold miners for the past several months. He even managed to steal from a few farmers as well as Mr. Moss over at the general store. The sheriff didn't have much success trying to capture this swindler."

"Then how'd you get him behind bars?" someone yelled from the audience.

"I'm getting to that," Ernie replied. "Seems we have some children in Miss Thompson's class who are mighty clever. These young folks devised a plan to capture the thief. A scoundrel named Abe Johnson found himself hanging upside down from Silas Smith's oak tree. And even more exciting is the fact that all of the gold and jewelry that was stolen has been recovered and returned to its rightful owners. Now you people know that getting stolen goods returned seldom happens. Anyway, we think these young folks need to be commended for what they've done."

Once again a burst of cheering and clapping erupted. "I would like to ask Yung Lee, Howard O'Laughlin, and the Smith children, John, Ben, and Lizzy to come up here on the stage," Mr. Sampson announced. The group looked back and forth among themselves, surprised by the adulation from the townsfolk, and slowly made their way to the stage.

A gasp could be heard from somewhere in the audience as Howard lifted Lee onto the stage. "What's he doing helping that yellow-skinned girl?" Mr. O'Laughlin muttered aloud.

"Don't pay him no never mind," Howard whispered. "He never learned to tolerate anything or anybody that's different."

"It's all right," Lee said, trying unsuccessfully to hide her embarrassment.

"I've asked these children to come up here because we have something special for them. Kind of a reward, you might say," Mr. Sampson told the audience. He held up five leather pouches. "These here each have gold nuggets in them. They were donated by the families who had their belongings safely returned." He proudly shook the children's hands as he gave each of them a reward. "Would any of you like to say anything?" he asked.

There was an uncomfortable silence, followed by Howard scuffing his shoe on the wooden platform. "I think I'd like to say something," Howard cautiously offered.

"Good!" Mr. Sampson heartily replied, pulling Howard forward.

"First of all, I sure don't deserve this," he said, raising the pouch above his head. "I didn't do anything. It was them that done it all," he continued, motioning toward the other children. "All I did was tell them how to set a good snare, and they did the rest. I'm sure glad it all worked out and that feller's locked up over at the jail." His comment brought another round of applause from the crowd. "But what I wanted to say has nothing to do with capturing that robber. I think most of you know that I'm not always the nicest person that lives in these parts." There were hoots and laughter from some of his old buddies who hadn't been promoted. "But that's changed," he said, raising his voice to be heard over their outburst.

"We liked you the way you were," one of the boys hollered.

"Well, I didn't," Howard replied as he shook his head. "During the last few months of school, Miss Thompson had one of the smarter kids help me with my lessons. She knew I wasn't going to pass my tests unless I had extra help. The person that helped me is this here little gal," he said. "This here is my very special friend, Yung Lee. She stayed in from recess and used her lunchtime to help me, even though I called her lots of ugly names and stole her teacup. So what I want to say is that she's the best friend I ever had. Lee taught me math and helped me with my essay, but the most important thing I learned from her is that how we look isn't really important. She showed me that if we'd start taking into account what folks are like on the inside instead of the outside, we'd get along a lot better. This here's a good example of that," he said, once again looking toward the other children on the stage. "I'm a white Irish boy; Lee's a yellow Chinese girl; Lizzy, Ben, and John are black African kids; but we all put our heads together and did a good thing for this town. I'm thinking that there are a lot of you who believe the same way that I used to—that anybody who don't look just like you can't be worth much. When you start thinking like that, I hope you'll remember what a bunch of different-looking kids accomplished when they quit looking at the outside and worked together."

There was a deafening silence. Even the flittering birds had ceased their singing. Howard stepped back beside Lee and gave her a halfhearted smile that broke into a wide grin as several people began clapping and were soon joined by others until the whole crowd was on their feet cheering.

"Would you look at that? Even my pa is clapping. It's hard to believe he might like what I had to say," Howard whispered to Lee, with a look of astonishment on his face.

"They all did, Howard. They liked it because what you said is the truth, and deep in their hearts they know it," she replied. "It was a wonderful speech."

"Thanks," he said. His freckled face had once again turned a crimson red that nearly matched his slicked-down hair. Giving Lee a smile, he lifted her off the stage to where the crowd was moving forward to congratulate and thank them.

Howard beamed as Mrs. Smith pulled him into a warm hug and thanked him for helping to end Abe Johnson's thieving ways. But Lee watched Howard stiffen as his father neared the front of the line. Mr. O'Laughlin had stood and clapped with the rest of the crowd, so Lee was confused by Howard's reaction. "Aren't you glad to see your pa? He's coming to congratulate you," Lee whispered.

"We'll see. That smile don't always mean he's happy. My pa's good at tricking me. He's fooled me plenty of times by putting a smile on his face. Then just about the time I think everything's okay, I feel the slap of his hand or the sting of his belt. But don't you pay no mind to anything he says to you. Ma says he was born ornery, and it ain't likely he's gonna change."

"People can change, Howard—look at you!" Lee declared.

Howard smiled and nodded his head in agreement. "That's true enough, but I had you praying for me and reminding me that Jesus loves me. I've been praying for my pa, but I don't think he'd take kindly to me telling him Jesus loves him," Howard replied as his father reached the front of the line.

Mr. O'Laughlin grabbed Howard's hand and began pumping his arm up and down. "I want to shake your hand, son. This here's the proudest day of my life, what with you passing to eighth grade and then getting this award for helping to do good. Makes me mighty proud, mighty proud."

"Thanks, Pa. I'm glad I've done something to please you," Howard cautiously replied.

Moving toward Lee, Mr. O'Laughlin looked down at the ground and shook his head. There was a long pause before he finally raised his head and met Lee's gaze. "I owe you an apology and a heap of thanks. My wife says I sometimes act like a dunderhead—guess she's right. I hope you can find it in your heart to forgive me. I've said some pretty mean things, and it took you kids to make me realize what a fool I've been.

You've done a lot to help my son, and if there's ever anything I can do in return, you just say the word!"

"Do you mean it?" Lee asked, with a sparkle in her eyes.

"Yes," Mr. O'Laughlin answered, a note of hesitation in his voice. "Didn't expect you'd need a favor quite so soon," he quickly added.

"It's not really a favor, but if you would like to do something that would make me happy, I would be very pleased if you and Mrs. O'Laughlin would bring Howard to church on Sundays. We have a good time, and I'm sure you and your wife would like the other families."

"Well, I dunno if the missus would want to be bothered getting out to church every Sunday, but ..."

"Oh, I'd love to attend church every Sunday. You know I've been after you for years to attend church," Mrs. O'Laughlin interjected as she moved forward and stood beside her husband.

"I guess that's true," he replied as a slow blush began to creep upward, turning his face a crimson shade that reminded Lee of Howard.

Lee gave him her sweetest smile. "Then we can count on seeing you in church on Sunday?"

Mr. O'Laughlin slowly nodded his head. "You've got my word. We'll be there. Guess we better move along and give the rest of these folks a chance to visit."

Howard turned toward Lee, his face etched in a look of disbelief. "I don't believe it. He's like a different person."

"We've all been praying for him. Guess we kind of ganged up on him," Lee replied, looking toward the three Smith children and giggling.

"Mama always says there's power in praying. We figured your pa would have to sweeten up if we were all praying for him," Lizzy explained. "Looks like it worked!"

"It sure does. Thank you," Howard said, giving them a big smile.

Strange, Lee thought to herself, that gap between Howard's front teeth doesn't seem nearly as noticeable as it did when I first met him. I wonder if I look any different to him?

Howard glanced up and caught her gazing at him. "What are you staring at?" he asked.

"Oh, nothing. I was just thinking about when I first met you."

"Seems like a long time ago, doesn't it? Hey, where's your brother? I haven't seen him this afternoon," Howard said when the crowd of well-wishers finally began to dwindle.

"I don't know. I haven't seen him since early this afternoon," Lee replied, her stomach beginning to churn.

Chapter Fourteen

Lee glanced back through the clustered groups of families and friends. She spotted the Smiths, who were visiting with Pastor Mitchell and his wife, but Fong wasn't with them. Surely he hadn't left. No, that would be impossible. After all, they had come in the Smiths' wagon, and it was too far to walk, wasn't it? Surely Fong wouldn't leave and walk home without saying anything to her.

"There he is!" Howard shouted, pointing toward a large cottonwood tree. Fong stood leaning against the gray, furrowed bark of the tree, while the tiny, egg-shaped pods fluttered down around him.

"I think I'll go and talk to him," Lee said. "He looks lonely."

Fong gave her an unexpected smile as she approached him. "What are you doing over here by yourself?" Lee asked.

"I don't know any of these people except the Smiths, and they are busy visiting with their friends. I don't want to intrude."

Lee shook her head and gave a small giggle. "These people wouldn't mind if you walked up to them and introduced yourself," Lee told him.

"Perhaps, but I'm comfortable over here by myself. I've been doing a lot of thinking."

"What about?" Lee asked.

"About how selfish I have been. I shouldn't have forced you to leave the Conroys and come to this country. It was unfair of me to make you leave everything you knew and loved. Finding gold was my dream, not yours. However, it does appear that you have made many friends and admirers. I'm very proud of you," he said in a hushed voice.

"Thank you," she replied, pleased with her brother's praise. "I know I've done things that have made you unhappy since we moved here. Like with the teacup . . ."

"But that worked out, and you ended up with a new friend. I shouldn't have gotten so upset with you. It wasn't your fault."

"Are you sorry that we came to America? You don't seem very happy, even though you and Mr. Smith have found gold," Lee asked, sitting down beside her brother on the lush bed of grass under the tree.

"It isn't what I expected—no streets of gold." They both laughed at that remark. "And even though Mr. Smith and I have found some gold, we'll have to find a lot more before I'd say we're successful. I thought it would be easier. I thought that I would find gold—that we'd be rich and could make a choice to live wherever and do whatever we wanted."

"Mrs. Conroy says people don't appreciate things unless they have to work for them. Maybe she's right. You probably wouldn't appreciate being rich if finding the gold was easy."

"Perhaps you're right. But I've decided that I'm going to search for only one more year. If we aren't rich by then, we'll return to China. You'll probably start praying that I won't find gold, won't you?" he asked.

"I don't think so. It isn't so bad here, but I would like to visit Chinatown again. I think that I might like to live there someday if you become rich. Living in Chinatown would allow us to live with our own people and still have American friends. Besides, Mr. and Mrs. Conroy are going to return to the United States in another year. Maybe we could visit them in Boston?" she asked, excitement filling her voice.

"First, I must find enough gold for all of this. I plan to save enough for our passage back to China just in case we decide to return."

"If not, can we use it for a trip to Boston?"

"You never give up, do you?" Fong asked, giving her a broad smile.

"Mrs. Conroy says I'm tenacious. That means stubborn. Mr. Smith says his mules are stubborn, so I think she must have been confused about that word."

"Oh, I don't think so," her brother said, giving her a hearty laugh as he pulled her into a giant bear hug. "You are every bit as stubborn as those mules of Mr. Smith's."

"That's for sure," Howard agreed as he came up to them. "I wanted to tell you that I'm sorry about the teacup. It wasn't Lee's fault." He extended his hand toward Fong. "We've never met before. I'm Howard."

Fong nodded. "Thank you for your apology, Howard. It's nice to meet you."

"Lee helped me a lot with my schoolwork. I guess you already know that," he said, blushing. "She even helped me after church one Sunday. I don't think I saw you there. Were you at church that Sunday when Lee studied with me?"

"No, I wasn't there. I don't attend church with Lee," Fong answered.

"You ought to come. My folks are gonna start coming this Sunday. Why don't you come, too? It could be a new beginning for all of us."

"Oh, yes. That would be wonderful. Would you?" Lee pleaded.

Fong couldn't help but laugh. "Now I have two tenacious children to contend with," he said. "I think I might as well agree. Otherwise, it will be a very long afternoon."

"Come here, come here!" Lee shouted to Lizzy and Mrs. Smith, who were standing a short distance away. "Guess what," she called as they drew a little closer.

"What?" Mrs. Smith asked. "It must be something very wonderful as excited as you look."

"Fong is going to come to church with us on Sunday," Lee bubbled with delight.

"Oh, that is wonderful news. I'm very pleased to hear that, Fong. I think you'll like church and all of the people, too," Mrs. Smith said. "Perhaps we should join the rest of the folks. Looks like they're beginning to serve lemonade and cookies."

The remainder of the afternoon passed in a flurry. There were refreshments, visiting, and music provided by Mr. Sampson's fiddle to keep everyone busy. It had been a wonderful day—everything Lee could have possibly hoped for, and more. She still couldn't believe that Howard had made such a wonderful speech to all those people and that his father had come and apologized for his unkind remark and had then thanked her for being Howard's tutor. Even more exciting was the fact that Mr. and Mrs. O'Laughlin were going to attend church. She had never expected all that to happen! All of those things plus her wonderful talk with Fong and his agreement to visit church next Sunday—it was almost too much to grasp.

"You gonna take your gold nuggets and go visit Mrs. Conroy in China?" Lizzy later whispered as they bounced along toward home in the wagon.

"No. Fong says he wants to search for gold one more year and see if he and your pa can find some great big nuggets. If not, he says we'll return to China or maybe even live in Chinatown. The Conroys will be returning to America in a year, and I'm hoping we can go and visit them in Boston. Besides, I promised Howard that I'd help him with his schoolwork next year. His pa doesn't want him to quit—said he wants him to graduate from eighth grade. I was thinking maybe I'd save my reward money to travel to Boston, just in case Fong doesn't strike it rich."

"Have you decided what you're going to do with your gold?" Lee asked Lizzy.

"I thought maybe I'd see if Ma would buy me a new pair of shoes. You know, some of those pretty pointy-toed ones like Mary Wilson wears instead of these," she replied, holding one of her shoes out toward Lee. "And maybe buy some material for new dresses for me and Ma. 'Course, we'd have to go to San Francisco to get the shoes. They don't carry nothing but these old heavy boots at the general store. But maybe we'll be going again come summer," she dreamily replied as the wagon pulled to a stop.

"Come on now. Let's get in the house," Mr. Smith called to the children. "You girls help with supper. I'm so hungry I could eat a mule."

Lee's eyes grew wide. "He's just kidding, Lee," Mrs. Smith said with a smile. "We need our mules too much to ever consider such a thing."

"Right! Besides, they'd probably taste mighty tough," Mr. Smith retorted, giving a hearty laugh.

Fong and Lee looked at each other and joined Mr. Smith in his laughter. "Maybe I shouldn't be quite so stubborn in the future," Lee whispered to her brother as he lifted her down from the wagon.

*　　*　　*

After dinner, Lee could hear John, Ben, and Lizzy shouting outdoors as they tried to catch fireflies. She sat at the table with her paper neatly spread in front of her as she began writing.

> *Dear Mrs. Conroy,*
> *Do you remember telling me that I would make new friends and my life in America would be a great adventure? You were right! Today was truly an amazing day....*